"The Best Course Is For Us To Be Married And Provide A Stable Home For The Baby."

"With two parents who can barely tolerate one another."

He raised one eyebrow. "I wouldn't go that far. I'd say we got on quite well together that night in my hotel room."

A deep flush worked its way over her cheeks. "Lust is no substitute for love, trust and commitment."

"And who is to say those things won't follow?"

She stared at him in astonishment.

"Give it a chance, Jewel. Who is to say what the future holds for us? Now, if we're finished, I suggest you get some rest. There are many things to be done, and the sooner I arrange everything, the sooner you can be at ease."

"I haven't said I'll marry you," she said evenly.

"No, and I'm waiting for your answer."

Dear Reader,

THE ANETAKIS TYCOONS trilogy comes to a close with *The Tycoon's Secret Affair,* Piers Anetakis's story. Of the three Anetakis brothers, Piers is the most closed off and the most troubled. But he's also the most passionate and emotional.

He's been hurt by past betrayals, but then so has Jewel Henley, the woman Piers meets one night in an intimate, tropical setting. These two are kindred spirits, and they have a lot to offer one another—if they can ever get around their issues of trust.

I'm inviting you along for the exciting conclusion of the Anetakis family's story. Rich, powerful and ruthless, these three men learn that no amount of wealth or privilege can ever fill the places in their hearts only love can reach. Piers and Jewel must navigate many obstacles in their search for happiness. Their love will be tested, and they'll have to offer the one thing not easily given by either: their trust.

Maya Banks

MAYA BANKS

THE TYCOON'S SECRET AFFAIR

Silhouette®

Desire

Published by Silhouette Books

America's Publisher of Contemporary Romance

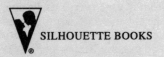

SILHOUETTE BOOKS

ISBN-13: 978-0-373-76960-5

Recycling programs
for this product may
not exist in your area.

THE TYCOON'S SECRET AFFAIR

Visit Silhouette Books at www.eHarlequin.com

Printed in U.S.A.

Books by Maya Banks

Silhouette Desire

The Tycoon's Pregnant Mistress #1920
The Tycoon's Rebel Bride #1944
The Tycoon's Secret Affair #1960

*The Anetakis Tycoons

MAYA BANKS

has loved romance novels from a very (very) early age, and almost from the start, she dreamed of writing them as well. In her teens, she filled countless notebooks with overdramatic stories of love and passion. Today her stories are only slightly less dramatic, but no less romantic.

She lives in Texas with her husband and three children, and wouldn't contemplate living anywhere other than the South. When she's not writing, she's usually hunting, fishing or playing poker. She loves to hear from readers, and she can be found online at either www.mayabanks.com or www.writemindedblog.com, or you can e-mail her at maya@mayabanks.com.

To Dee, who loved Piers from the start.

Prologue

Jewel Henley shifted on the hospital bed, one hand curled around her cell phone, the other hand pushing aside hot tears. She had to call him. She had no choice.

Having to depend on the man who couldn't get her out of his life fast enough after their one-night stand wasn't a prospect she relished, but for her baby, she'd do anything. Swallow her pride and try to let go of the burning anger.

Her free hand dropped to rest on the burgeoning swell of her belly, and she felt the sturdy reassurance of her daughter's kick.

How would Piers react when she told him he was going to be a father? Would he even care? She shook her head in mute denial. Surely, no matter his feelings for her, he wouldn't turn his back on his child.

There was only one way to find out and that was to push

the send button. His private phone number was already punched in. She may have been fired from her job, but for some reason, she'd held on to the phone numbers she'd been provided upon her hiring.

And still she couldn't bring herself to complete the call. She let the phone drop to her chest and closed her eyes. If only there weren't complications with her pregnancy. Why couldn't she be one of these beautiful, glowing women who were pictures of health?

Her thoughts were interrupted when her door swung open and a nurse bustled in pushing a cart with the computer she used to log her charts.

"How are you feeling today, Miss Henley?"

Jewel nodded and whispered a faint, "Fine."

"Have you made arrangements for your care after your release?"

Jewel swallowed but didn't say anything. The nurse gave her a reproving look.

"You know the doctor won't release you until he's satisfied that you'll have someone to look after you while you're on bed rest."

A sigh escaped Jewel's lips and she held up the phone. "I was just about to make a call."

The nurse nodded approvingly. "Good. As soon as I'm done I'll leave you alone to finish."

A few minutes later the nurse left, and once again Jewel lifted the phone and stared at the LCD screen. Maybe he wouldn't even answer.

Taking a deep, fortifying breath, she punched her thumb over the send button then closed her eyes and put the phone to her ear. There was a brief silence as the call connected, and then it began to ring.

Once. Twice. Then a third time. She was preparing to

chicken out and cut the connection when his brusque voice filled her ear.

"Anetakis."

It came out more of a growl than anything else, and she quickly lost courage. Her breath came stuttering out as more tears welled in her eyes.

"Who is this?" he demanded.

She yanked the phone away and clumsily jabbed at the buttons until the call ended. She couldn't do this. Issuing a silent apology to her unborn baby, she decided that she'd find another way. There had to be something she could do that didn't involve Piers Anetakis.

Before she could dwell too long on such possibilities, the phone pulsed in her hand. She opened it automatically, a second before she realized that he was calling her back.

Only her soft breathing spilled into the receiver.

"I know you're there," Piers barked. "Now who the hell is this and how did you get my number?"

"I'm sorry," she said in a low voice. "I shouldn't have bothered you."

"Wait," he commanded. Then there was a long pause. "Jewel, is that you?"

Oh God. She hadn't counted on him recognizing her voice. How could he? They hadn't spoken in five months. Five months, one week and three days to be exact.

"Y-yes," she finally said.

"Thank God," he muttered. "I've been looking everywhere for you. Just like a damn female to disappear off the face of the earth."

"What?"

"Where are you?"

The questions came simultaneously.

"Me first," he said imperiously. "Where are you? Are you all right?"

She laid there in stunned silence before she gathered her scattered wits. "I'm in the hospital."

"Theos." There was another rapid smattering of Greek that she couldn't have followed even if she understood the language.

"Where?" he bit out. "What hospital? Tell me."

Completely baffled at the turn the conversation had taken, she told him the name of the hospital. Before she could say anything else, he cut in with, "I'll be there as soon as I can."

And then the line went dead.

With shaking hands, she folded the phone shut and set it aside. Then she curled her fingers around the bulge of her abdomen. He was coming? Just like that? He'd been looking for her? None of it made sense.

Then she realized that she'd never told him the most important piece of information. The entire reason she'd called him to begin with. She hadn't told him she was pregnant.

One

Jewel paused just outside the perimeter of the outdoor bar and stared over the sand-covered floor to the blazing torches lining the walkway down to the beach.

Music played softly, a perfect accompaniment to the clear, star-strung night. In the distance, the waves rolled in harmony with the sultry melody. Soft jazz. Her favorite.

It was pure chance that had directed her to this tiny island paradise. A vacated seat on a plane, a bargain ticket price and only five minutes to decide. And here she was. A new place, a vow to take a few days for herself.

Not being completely impulsive, the first thing she'd done when she'd arrived was to find a new temporary job, and as luck would have it, had learned that the owner of the opulent Anetakis hotel was going to be in temporary residence here and needed an assistant. Four weeks. A perfect amount of time to spend in paradise before she moved on.

The opportunity had almost been too good to be true. Along with a generous salary, she'd also been given a room at the hotel. It had the makings of a marvelous vacation.

"Are you going out or are you going to spend such a lovely night indoors?"

The vaguely accented male voice brushed across her ears, eliciting a trail of chill bumps down her spine. She turned and was forced to look up for the source of the huskily spoken words.

When she met his eyes, she felt the impact clear to her toes. Her belly clenched, and for a moment it was hard to breathe.

The man wasn't just gorgeous. There were plenty of gorgeous men in the world, and she'd met her share. This one was…powerful. A predator in a sea of sheep. His eyes bore into hers with an intensity that almost frightened her.

There was interest. Clear interest. She wasn't a fool, nor did she indulge in silly games of false modesty.

She stared back, unable to wrest herself from the force of his gaze. Black. His eyes were as black as night. His hair was as dark, and his skin gleamed golden brown in the soft light of the torches. Firelight cast a sheen to his eyes, shiny onyx, glittering and proud.

His jawline was firm, set, a strong tilt that denoted his arrogance, a quality she was attracted to in men. For a long moment he returned her frank appraisal, and then his lips curved upward into a slight smile.

"A woman of few words I see."

She shook herself and mentally scolded her tongue for knotting up so badly.

"I was deciding on whether to go out or not."

He lifted one imperious brow, a gesture that seemed more challenging than questioning.

"But I can't buy you a drink if you remain inside."

She cocked her head to the side, allowing a tiny smile to relax the tension bubbling inside her. She wasn't a stranger to sexual attraction, but she couldn't remember the last time a man had affected her so strongly right off the bat.

Awareness sizzled between them, almost as if a fuse had been lit the moment he'd spoken. Would she accept the unspoken invitation in his eyes? Oh, she knew he'd asked to buy her a drink, but that wasn't all he wanted. The question was whether she was bold enough to reach out and take the offer.

What could a single night hurt? She was extremely choosy in her partners. She hadn't taken a lover in two years. She just hadn't been interested until this dark-eyed stranger with his sensual smile and mocking arrogance came along. Oh yes, she wanted him. So much so that she vibrated with it.

"Are you here on holiday?" she asked as she peered up at him from underneath her lashes.

Again his lips quirked into a half smile. "In a manner of speaking."

Relief scurried through her belly. No, one night wouldn't hurt. He'd leave and go back to his world. Eventually she'd move on, and their paths would never cross again.

Tonight…tonight she was lonely, a feeling she didn't often indulge in, even if she spent the majority of her time in isolation.

"I'd like a drink," she said by way of agreement.

Something predatory sparked in his eyes. A glow that

was gone almost as soon as it burst to life. His hand came up and cupped her elbow, his fingers splaying possessively over her skin.

She closed her eyes for a brief moment, enjoying the electric sensation that sizzled through her body the moment he touched her.

He led her from the protective awning of the hotel into the night air. Around them the warm glow of torches danced in time with the sweet sounds of jazz. The breeze coming off the water blew through her hair, and she inhaled deeply, enjoying the salt tang.

"Dance with me before we have that drink," he murmured close to her ear.

Without waiting for her consent, he pulled her into his arms, his hips meeting hers as he cupped her body close.

They fit seamlessly, her flush against him, melting and flowing until she wasn't sure where she ended and he began.

His cheek rested against the side of her head as his arms encircled her. Protective. Strong. She reached up, sliding her arms over his shoulders until they wrapped around his neck.

"You're beautiful."

His words flowed like warm honey over jaded ears. It wasn't the most original line, but that was just it. Coming from him, it didn't sound like a line, but rather an honest assessment, a sincere compliment, one that maybe he'd ordinarily be unwilling to give.

"So are you," she whispered.

He chuckled, and his laughter vibrated over her sensitive skin. "Me beautiful? I'm unsure of whether to be flattered or offended."

She snorted. "I know for a fact I'm not the only woman to have ever called you beautiful."

"Do you now?"

His hands skimmed over her back, finding the flesh bared by the backless scoop of her dress. She sucked in her breath as his fingers burned her flesh.

"You feel it too," he murmured.

She didn't pretend not to know what he meant. The chemistry between them was combustible. Never before had she experienced anything like this, not that she'd tell him that.

Instead she nodded her agreement.

"Are we going to do anything about it?"

She leaned back and tilted her head to meet his eyes. "I'd like to think we are."

"Direct. I like that in a woman."

"I like that in a man."

Amusement softened the intensity of his gaze, but she saw something else in his expression. Desire. He wanted her as badly as she wanted him.

"We could have that drink in my room."

She sucked in her breath. Even though she knew what he wanted, the invitation still hit her squarely in the stomach. Her breasts tightened against his chest, and arousal bloomed deep.

"I'm not…" For the first time, she sounded unsure, hesitant. Not at all the decisive woman she knew herself to be.

"You're not what?" he prompted.

"Protected," she said, her voice nearly drowning in the sounds around them.

He tucked a finger underneath her chin and forced her to once again meet his seeking gaze. "I'll take care of you."

The firm promise wrapped around her more securely than his arms. For a moment she indulged in the fantasy of what it would be like to have a man such as this take care of her for the rest of her life. Then she shook her head. Such foolish notions shouldn't disrupt the fantasy of this one night.

She rose up on tiptoe, her lips a breath away from his. "What's your room number?"

"I'll take you up myself."

She shook her head, and he frowned.

"I'll meet you there."

His eyes narrowed for a moment as if he wasn't sure whether to believe her or not. Then without warning, he slid a hand around her neck and curled his fingers around her nape. He pulled her to him, pressing his lips to hers.

She went liquid against him, her body sliding bonelessly downward. He hauled her against him with his free arm, anchoring her tight to prevent her fall.

He licked over her lips, pressing, demanding her to open. With a breathless gasp, she surrendered, parting her mouth so his tongue could slide inward.

Hot, moist open-mouthed kisses. He stole her breath and returned it. His teeth scraped at her lip then captured it and tugged relentlessly. Unwilling to remain a passive participant, she fired back, sucking at his tongue.

His groan echoed over her ears. Her sigh spilled into his mouth.

He finally pulled away, his breaths coming in ragged heaves. His eyes flashed dangerously, sending a shiver over her flesh.

Then he shoved a keycard into her hand. "Top floor. Suite eleven. Hurry."

With that he turned and stalked back into the hotel, his stride eating up the floor.

She stared after him, her body humming and her mind

in a million different pieces. She was completely shattered by what she'd just experienced.

"I must be insane. He'll eat me alive."

A low hum of heady desire buzzed through her veins. She could only hope she was right.

She turned on shaking legs and walked slowly into the hotel. It wasn't that she was being deliberately coy by putting her mystery man off. Mystery man… She didn't even know his name, but she'd agreed to have sex with him.

Then again, it had a certain appeal, this air of mystery. A night of fantasy. No names. No expectations. No entanglements or emotional involvement. No one would get hurt. It was, in fact, perfect.

No, she wasn't being cute. But if she was going to go through with this, it would be on her own terms. Her dark-eyed lover wouldn't have complete control of the situation.

With more calm than she felt, she went up to her room. Once there, she surveyed her reflection in the bathroom mirror. Her hair was slightly mussed and her lips swollen. Passion. She looked as if she'd had an encounter with the very essence of passion.

The sultry temptress staring back at her wasn't a woman she recognized, but she decided she liked this new person. She looked beautiful and confident, and excitement sparked her eyes at the thought of what waited for her in suite eleven.

After a lifetime of loneliness, of being alone, the idea of spending the night in a lover's arms was so appealing that it was all she could do not to hurry out to the elevator.

Instead she forced herself to take steadying breaths. She stared at herself until the wildness faded from her eyes and coolness replaced it. Then she smoothed her long blond hair away from her face.

Satisfied that she had herself under control, she walked out of the bathroom to sit on the bed. She'd wait fifteen to twenty minutes before she headed up. No need to seem too eager.

Two

Piers prowled his suite, unaccustomed to the edginess that consumed him ever since he'd parted ways with the blond bombshell downstairs. He stopped his restless pacing and poured a drink from the crystal decanter on the bar, but he didn't drink it. Instead he stared at the amber liquid then glanced at his watch for the third time.

Would she come?

He cursed his eagerness. He felt like an errant teenager sneaking out of the house to meet a girlfriend. His reaction to the woman couldn't be explained except in terms of lust and desire.

He wanted her. Had wanted her from the moment he spotted her staring longingly through the open doorway of the hotel. He'd been mesmerized by the picture she portrayed. Long and sleek with slender legs, a narrow waist and high, firm breasts. Her hair fell like silk over her shoulders and down her back and his fingers itched to dive into the tresses and wrap them around his knuckles while he devoured her plump lips.

Even now his groin ached uncomfortably. Never had he reacted so strongly to a woman, and it bothered him even as the idea of taking her to bed fired his senses.

A soft knock at his door thrust him to attention, and he hurried across to open it. She stood there, delightfully shy, her ocean eyes a strange mixture of emerald and sapphire.

"I know you gave me a key," she said in a low voice, "but it seemed rude to just barge in."

He found his voice, though his mouth had gone dry as soon as she spoke. He reached for her hand, and she placed it trustingly in his. "I'm glad you came," he said huskily as he pulled her forward.

Instead of leading her farther inside, he wrapped his arms around her, molding her to the contours of his body. She trembled softly against him, and he could feel her heart fluttering like the beat of hummingbird wings.

Unable to resist the temptation, he lowered his mouth to hers, wanting to taste her again. Just once. But when their lips met, he forgot all about his intention to sample.

She responded hotly, her arms sliding around his body. Her hands burned into his skin, through the material of his shirt as if it wasn't there. His impatience grew. He wanted her naked. Wanted him to be naked so he could feel her skin on his.

Thoughts of taking it slow, of seducing her in measured steps flew out the window as he drank deeply of her sweetness. He wasn't sure who was seducing whom, and at this moment, it didn't matter.

His lips scorched a path down the side of her neck as his fingers tugged impatiently at the fastenings of her dress.

Smooth, creamy skin revealed itself, and his mouth was drawn relentlessly to the bare expanse as her dress fell away.

She moaned softly and shivered as his tongue trailed over the curve of her shoulder. He pushed at the dress, and it fell to the floor leaving her in only a dainty scrap of lacy underwear.

All his breath left him as he looked down at the full round globes of her breasts. Her nipples puckered and strained as if begging for his attention. The tips were velvet under his seeking fingers. He toyed with one and then the other before cupping one breast in his palm and lowering his head to press a kiss just above the peach areola.

Her breath caught and held, and she tensed as his tongue lazily traced downward to suck the nipple into his mouth.

Her taste exploded in his mouth. Sweet. Delicate like a flower. So feminine. Perfect. His senses reeled, and he pulled away for a moment to recoup his control. *Theos* but she drove him mad. He reacted to her like a man making love to his first woman.

Already his manhood strained at his pants, and he was dangerously close to flinging her on the bed and stroking into her liquid heat.

Finesse. He must take it slower. He wouldn't allow her such power over him. He would make her as crazy as she made him, and then and only then would he take her.

Jewel grabbed his shoulders as her knees buckled. She needn't have worried. He swept her into his arms and carried her toward the bedroom just beyond the sitting area of the suite.

He laid her on the bed then stood back and began to hastily strip out of his clothing. There was something incredibly sexy about a man standing over her as he undressed. His eyes burned into her, heating her skin even from a distance.

First his shirt fell away revealing smooth, muscled shoulders, a rugged chest and narrow waist with enough of a six-pack to suggest he wasn't an idle businessman. Hair dotted the hollow of his chest, spreading just to his flat nipples. It was thicker at his midline, trailing lower to his navel, tapering to a faint smattering just above the waist of his pants.

She stared hungrily at him as he unfastened his trousers. He didn't waste time or tease unnecessarily. He shoved them down his legs, taking his boxers with him. His erection sprang free from a dark nest of hair. Her eyes widened at the way it strained upward, toward his taut belly. He was hugely aroused.

Her question must have shone on her face. He crawled onto the bed, straddling her hips with his knees. "Was there any doubt that I wanted you, *yineka mou?*"

She smiled up at him. "No."

"Rest assured, I want you very much," he said huskily. He lowered his head until his mouth found hers in a heated rush.

Her entire body arched to meet him, wanting the contact, the warmth and passion he offered. It had been so long since she'd purposely sought out the company of another person, and this man assaulted her senses. He flooded her with a longing that unsettled her.

He pushed her arms over her head until she was helpless beneath him. He didn't just kiss her, he devoured her. There wasn't an inch of her skin that didn't feel the velvet brush of his lips.

Her gasp echoed across the room when he licked and

suckled each breast in turn. His tongue left a damp trail down her midline as he licked down to the shallow indention of her navel. There wasn't a single muscle that wasn't quivering in sharp anticipation.

His hands followed, his palms running the length of her body, tracing each curve, each indention on they settled on her hips. He tucked his thumbs underneath the thin string holding her underwear in place, and then he pressed his mouth to her soft mound still covered by transparent lace.

She cried out softly, unnerved by the electric sensation of his mouth over her most intimate place, and yet he hadn't even made contact with her flesh.

His hands caressed their way down her legs, dragging the underwear with it. At her knees, he simply ripped impatiently, rending the material in two. He quickly discarded it and returned impatient fingers to her thighs.

Carefully, he spread her, and she began to shake in earnest.

"Don't be afraid," he murmured. "I'll take care of you. Trust me tonight. You're so beautiful. I want to give you the sweetest pleasure."

"Yes. Please, yes," she begged.

He kissed the inside of her knee. With a brush of his lips, he moved higher, kissing the inside of her thigh, and then finally brushing over the curls guarding her most sensitive regions.

With a gentle finger, he parted her. "Give me your pleasure, *yineka mou*. Only to me." And then his mouth touched her. She bucked upward with a wild cry as his tongue delved deep. It was too much. It had been too long. Never had she reacted so strongly to a man.

"So responsive. So wild. I can't wait to have you."

He rolled away, and she gave a sharp protest until she saw he was only putting on a condom. Then he was back, spreading her thighs, stroking her to make sure she was ready for him.

"Take me. Make me yours," she pleaded.

He closed his eyes, his fingers tight at her hips. He spread her wide and surged into her with one hard thrust.

Her shocked gasp spilled from her lips. Her fingers tightened at his shoulders, and she lay still, simply absorbing the rugged sensation of having him inside her.

His eyes flew open. "Did I hurt you?" he demanded harshly, the strain evident on his face as he held himself in check.

She touched his cheek, trying to soften the lines. His eyes glittered dangerously, and she realized just how close he was to the edge of his control. In that moment, she relished her power, and she wanted to taunt the beast. She wanted to experience the wildness she could see lurking beyond the iron facade.

"No," she said softly. "You didn't hurt me. I want you so much. Take me now. Don't hold back."

To emphasize her request, she dug her nails into his shoulders then lifted her hips in a move that lodged him deeper inside her.

He made one last effort to hold back, but she wouldn't allow it. Wrapping her legs tightly around his waist, she arched into him, reaching for him, pulling him closer. She wanted him. She *needed* him.

He dropped down, surrendering with a growl. He gathered her close, fastening his lips to the vulnerable skin of her neck as his body took over. Harder and faster, his power overwhelmed her. There was a delicious mix of erotic pain and sensual bliss. Heaven. It wasn't something she'd ever experienced before. It was like riding a hurricane.

"Let go," he rasped in her ear. "You first."

She complied without argument, surrendering completely to his will. Her orgasm flashed, terrifying and thrilling all at the same time. She spun wildly out of control, her cries mixing with his.

Then he was moving faster, and harder, driving into her with savage intensity. His lips fused to hers almost in a desperate attempt to staunch his own sounds, but they escaped, harsh and masculine.

Then he stilled inside her, his hips trembling uncontrollably against hers. He smoothed his hands, now gentle, over her face, through her hair and then he gathered her close, murmuring words she didn't understand against her ear.

When his weight grew too heavy, he shifted to the side, pulling her into his arms. He slipped from the warm grasp of her body then rolled away from her for a moment to discard the condom.

She waited with breathless anticipation. Would he want her to leave now or would he want her to spend the night? She was too sated and boneless to even think about getting up, but neither did she want any awkward situations.

He answered her unspoken dilemma by pulling her back into his arms and tucking her head underneath his chin. A few moments later, his soft breathing blew through her hair. He had fallen asleep.

Cautiously so as not to awaken him, she curled her arm around his waist and snuggled deeper into his embrace. Her cheek rested against the hair-roughened skin of his chest, and she inhaled deeply, filling her nostrils with his male scent.

For the space of a stolen moment she felt safe. Accepted. Even cherished. It was silly if she dwelled on it, but tonight she wouldn't. Tonight she just wanted to belong to someone and not to feel so alone in the world.

Even in sleep, he seemed to sense her disquiet. His arms tightened around her, bringing her even closer to his warmth. She smiled and gave in to the sleepy pleasure seeping into her bones.

Piers awoke unsure of the time, a rarity for him. He usually woke every morning before dawn, his mind alert and ready to take on the day's tasks. Today however sleep clouded his brain, and uncharacteristic laziness permeated his muscles. Something soft and feminine stirred his senses, and he woke enough to realize that she was still in his arms.

Instead of rolling away, of distancing himself immediately, he remained there, breathing in her scent. He should get up and shower, make it clear the interlude was over, but he hung on, unwilling to send her away just yet.

She stirred when his hands smoothed over her back, down to her shapely buttocks and over the curve of her hip. He had to have her again. One more time. Even as warning bells clanged in his mind, he was turning her, sliding over her as he reached to the nightstand for another condom.

As her eyes fluttered sleepily, he slid inside her, slower this time, with more patience and care than he'd taken her the night before. He didn't want to chance hurting her, and if he was honest, he wanted to savor this last encounter.

"Good morning," she murmured in a husky voice that sent a shudder over his body.

He thrust deeper then leaned down to capture her mouth. "Good morning."

She yawned and stretched like a cat, wrapping her arms

around his neck to pull him down again when he drew away. Sleek and beautiful, she matched his movements, rocking gently against him.

If last night had been the storm, this was a calm rain afterward. Gentle and extremely satisfying.

He tugged her hair from her face, unable to resist kissing her again and again. He couldn't get enough of her. The thought that he didn't want her to go rose in his mind. Before it could take root, he tamped it back down, determined not to get caught in an emotional trap.

He'd existed for too long without such entanglements, and he'd be damned if he allowed it to happen again.

She enveloped him in her tight grasp, her sweet depths clinging to him as he withdrew and thrust forward. He set an easy pace, one that would prolong their pleasure.

And when he could no longer delay the surge of exquisite pleasure, he pushed them both over the edge, leaving them gasping for breath and shaking in each other's arms.

For a long moment he lay there, still sheathed deeply inside her, his face buried in her sweet-smelling hair.

Then reality encroached. It was morning. Their night together was over, and it was best to end things now before things had a chance to get messy.

He rolled away abruptly, getting up from the bed and reaching for his pants.

"I'm going to take a shower," he said shortly when she did nothing more than watch him from her perch in his bed, her eyes probing him with a wary light.

She nodded, and he disappeared into the bathroom, his relief not as great as his regret. And when he returned a mere ten minutes later, he found her gone from his bed, from his hotel room. From his life.

Yes, she'd understood well the rules of the game.

Maybe too well. For a moment he'd allowed himself to wish that maybe, just maybe she'd still be lying there. Warm and sated from his lovemaking. Belonging to him.

Three

Jewel stood outside the third floor offices of the Anetakis Hotel and smoothed a hand through her hair for the third time. It was a bad nervous habit and one destined to bring down more tendrils from the elegant knot she'd fashioned.

Instead she placed her palms over her skirt and removed nonexistent wrinkles as she waited admittance into Piers Anetakis's office.

She knew she looked cool and professional, a look she strove hard for. The woman who'd let loose with such abandon two nights before no longer existed. In her place was an unreadable face devoid of any emotion.

Still, despite her best efforts, thoughts of her lover drifted erotically through her mind. She'd left while he was in the shower, but she'd hoped to run into him again. A chance meeting. Maybe it would lead to another night even though she'd sworn it would only be one.

It was just as well. He was probably already gone back to wherever it was he lived. She'd move on herself in a few more weeks, armed with enough money to sustain her travels.

At times, she wondered what it would be like to settle in one place, to have all the comforts of home, but such an idea was alien to her. She'd learned long ago that a home wasn't in the cards for her.

She glanced down at her watch. Two minutes past eight. She was to have been summoned at eight. Apparently promptness wasn't one of Mr. Anetakis's strong points.

She clutched her briefcase to her and stared out the window to the waves crashing in the distance. The sea lost some of its romance in the daylight. It was still beautiful and striking, but at night under the flicker of torches and the glow of the moon, it took on a life of its own.

Her mouth twisted ruefully. She was still thinking of her dark-eyed lover. He was hard to forget, and she knew she'd be thinking of him for a long time to come.

Behind her the door opened, and an older woman stuck her head out and smiled at Jewel. "Miss Henley, Mr. Anetakis will see you now."

Jewel pasted a bright smile on her face and marched in behind the woman. Across the room Mr. Anetakis stood with his back to them, a cell phone stuck to his ear. When he heard them come in, he turned and Jewel halted. Her mouth flew open, and her eyes widened in shock.

To his credit, Mr. Anetakis merely raised an eyebrow in recognition, and then he closed his phone and nodded to the other lady.

"You can leave us now, Margery. Miss Henley and I have a lot to discuss."

Jewel swallowed nervously as Margery quietly left the room and shut the door behind her. Her fingers curled around her briefcase, and she held it almost like a shield as Mr. Anetakis stared holes through her. God, how this must look.

"You have to know I had no idea who you were," she said in a shaky voice before he could speak.

"Indeed," he said calmly. "I could see the shock when I turned around. Still, it makes things a bit awkward, wouldn't you say?"

"There's no reason things should be awkward," she said crisply. She moved forward, holding an outstretched hand. "Hello, Mr. Anetakis. I'm Jewel Henley, your new assistant. I trust we'll work well together."

His lips twisted into a sardonic smile. Before he could reply, his phone rang again.

"Excuse me, Miss Henley," he said in a cool voice. Then he picked up his cell phone.

He wasn't speaking English, but it was obvious the phone call wasn't to his liking. He frowned and then outright scowled. He barked a few words into the receiver before muttering something unintelligible and snapping it closed.

"My apologies. There is something I must attend to at once. You can see Margery in her office, and she'll get you…set up."

Jewel nodded as he strode out the door. As soon as the door shut, all her breath left her in a whoosh that left her sagging. Of all the rotten luck. And to think she'd hoped they'd run into each other again so they could have a repeat performance.

On wobbly knees she went to find Margery and then prayed that she'd get through the next four weeks without losing her composure.

Piers got out of the helicopter and strode toward the car waiting to pick him up. As they drove toward the airport where his private jet awaited, he snapped open his phone and placed the call that he'd been deliberating over since he left his office.

His human resources manager for the island hotel picked up on the second ring.

"What can I do for you, Mr. Anetakis?" he asked once Piers had identified himself.

"Jewel Henley," he bit out.

"Your new assistant?"

"Get rid of her."

"Pardon? Is there a problem?"

"Just get rid of her. I want her gone by the time I return." He took a deep breath. "Transfer her, promote her or pay her for the entirety of her contract, but get rid of her. She can't work under me. I have a strict policy about personal involvement with my employees, and let's just say she and I have history."

He waited for a moment and when he didn't hear anything, he said, "hello?" He cursed. The connection had been cut. Oh well, he didn't require a response. He just wanted action.

Even if he hadn't already been extremely distrustful of situations that seemed too coincidental, his brother's assistant had sold valuable company plans to their competitor. After that debacle, they'd all assumed very strict requirements for the people working closest to them. They could ill afford another Roslyn.

Still, his chest tightened as the car stopped outside his plane, and he got out to board. He wasn't so much in denial that he could refute that the night had been more than just a casual one-night stand. Which was all the more reason to cut ties now. He wouldn't give up any power, no matter how subtle, to a woman ever again.

* * *

Jewel sat in Margery's chair behind her desk filling out a mountain of paperwork while Margery puttered around in the background making phone calls and grumbling at the printer when it didn't spit out the appropriate documents.

She'd spent the morning on pins and needles, waiting for Piers to return so they could at least try and air things out and get it behind them. The old saying about an elephant in the room was appropriate, only Jewel felt like there was an entire herd.

At lunch, she went down to the small café and nibbled on a sandwich while watching the seagulls dive-bomb tourists who had bread to feed them. If Margery let her on the company computer this afternoon, she'd e-mail Kirk and let him know she'd arrived on the island and would be staying a few weeks.

He was her only friend, but they rarely saw each other. He was forever taking assignments to far-flung places, and she was equally determined to travel her own way. It amused her that they were essentially lost souls who wandered from place to place. Neither had a home, and maybe that was why they understood each other.

An occasional e-mail, sometimes a phone call, and every once in a while they crossed paths on their travels. Those were good times. It was nice to connect to another person even if it was only for a few hours. He was as close to a brother or family member as she'd ever imagined having.

After finishing her sandwich, she tossed the wrapper and walked back to the employee elevator. Would Piers be back? A flutter abounded in her stomach, but she swallowed back her nervousness and forged ahead. It wouldn't do to let him know she was put off by their unintentional relationship. If he could be cool about it then so could she.

When she walked back into Margery's office, Margery looked up, a grim expression on her face. "Mr. Patterson wants to see you immediately."

Jewel's brow crinkled. Maybe it was more personnel stuff to sign. Lord knows she'd had enough paperwork this morning to choke a horse. With a resigned sigh, she turned and left Margery's office and went several doors down to the human resource manager's cubicle.

He looked up when she tapped on the frame of his open door.

"Miss Henley, come in. Have a seat please."

She settled down in front of him and waited expectantly. He cleared his throat and tugged at his collar in an uncomfortable motion. Then he leveled a stare at her.

"When you hired on, it was with the condition that it was a temporary position. You were to be Mr. Anetakis's assistant for the duration of his stay here."

"Yes." They'd been through all of this and she was impatient to get on with it.

"I'm sorry to say that he no longer requires an assistant. He's had a change of plans. As such, your services are no longer required."

She stared, stunned, for a long moment. "Excuse me?"

"Your employment here is terminated effective immediately."

She stood, her legs trembling, her fingers curled into tight fists. "That bastard. What a complete and utter bastard!"

"Security will escort you to your room and wait while you collect your things," he continued as if she hadn't let loose with her tirade.

"You can tell Mr. Anetakis that he is the lowest form of pond scum. Verbatim, Mr. Patterson. Make sure he gets my message. He's a gutless piece of chicken shit, and I hope he chokes on his damn cowardice."

With that she turned and stormed out of his office, slamming the door as hard as she could. The sound reverberated down the hallway, and a few people stuck their heads out of their cubicles as she stalked past.

Unbelievable. He hadn't even had the courage to fire her himself. He let his personnel director handle it while he ran for the hills. What a crock.

Two security guards fell into step beside her when she neared the elevator. It pissed her off that she was being treated like a common criminal.

She rode the elevator with them in stiff silence. They walked behind her to her door and positioned themselves on either side of the frame while she went in. How long would they give her before bursting in? The thought amused her even as rage crawled over her in waves.

Shedding her uncomfortable heels, she sank onto the bed like a deflated balloon. Damn the man. She had enough money to get off the island, but little else. Certainly no money to plan her next venture. She'd spent what she had to get here and taken the good-paying job to restock her resources. With the money earned in this job, she would have been able to travel, albeit economically, for the next six months without worrying about finances.

Now she faced the only choice available to her if she wanted a roof over her head. Going back home to San Francisco and the apartment that belonged to Kirk was her only option.

It had been an agreement between them. If she ever needed a place to stay, she was to go there. The utilities were taken care of each month and the pantry was stocked with staples.

She didn't even have a way to contact him other than e-mail, and sometimes he went weeks without checking it. She just hoped he hadn't planned one of his rare trips home at the same time she'd be there.

Her fingers dug into her temples, and she closed her eyes. She could look for work here on the island, but she'd already exhausted most of her possibilities when this job had landed in her lap. Nothing else paid nearly as well, and now she had no desire to stay where she might actually run into Piers Anetakis. The worm.

San Francisco was it, she admitted with forlorn acceptance. Hopefully she could land a job, save up some money. Having a rent-free place to stay would be helpful but she hated to take advantage of Kirk's generosity.

"Damn you, Piers Anetakis," she whispered. He'd managed to turn the most beautiful night of her life into something tawdry and hateful.

With a resigned shake of her head, she knew there was little point in feeling sorry for herself. There was nothing to do but pick up and go on and hopefully learn a lesson in the process.

Four

Five months later...

Piers descended the steps of his private jet and strode across the paved runway to the waiting car. The damp, chilly San Francisco air was a far cry from the warm, tropical air he was used to. He hadn't taken the time to pack appropriate clothing, and the thin silk shirt and light suit coat didn't offer much in the way of protection from the pervading chill.

The driver had already been instructed as to Piers's destination, so he sat back as the car rolled away from the airport toward the hospital where Jewel was being treated.

What had happened to her? It must be serious if she'd broken down and phoned him after he hadn't been able to uncover her whereabouts for five months. Guilt was a strong motivator, and yet his efforts had come to naught.

No matter. He now knew where she was. He'd see to it

that she had the best care and settle an amount on her to compensate her loss of employment, and then maybe he could get her out of his head.

When they finally rolled up to the hospital, Piers wasted no time hurrying in. At the help desk he was given Jewel's room number, and he rode the elevator to the appropriate floor.

At her door, he found it slightly ajar and issued a soft knock. Not hearing any summons, he pushed the door open and quietly walked in.

She was barely more than a rumpled pile of sheets on the bed, her head propped haphazardly on her pillow. Her eyelashes rested on her cheeks, and her soft, even breathing signaled her sleep.

Even in rest, she looked worried, her face drawn, her brow wrinkled. Her fingers were clutched bloodlessly at the sheet gathered at her chest. And yet she was as beautiful as he remembered, and unfortunately for him, he'd been haunted by her beauty for the last five months.

He removed his suit coat and tossed it over the chair beside her bed and then settled himself down to sit and wait for her to wake. The slight movement alerted her, and her eyes flew open.

Shock registered as soon as she saw him. Her eyes widened in what looked to be panic. Her hands moved immediately to her stomach in a protective gesture he'd be blind to miss.

Then he saw what it was she was protecting. There was an unmistakable swell, a taut mound that shielded a baby!

"You're pregnant!"

Her eyes narrowed. "Well, you needn't sound so accusing. I hardly got that way by myself."

For a moment he was too stunned to realize her implication, and then when it came, it trickled like ice down his spine. Old memories came back in a wave, and hot anger quickly melted away the cold in his veins.

"Are you saying it's mine?" he demanded. Already his mind was moving in a whir. He wouldn't be trapped again by a conniving woman.

"She," Jewel corrected. "At least refer to your daughter as a human being."

Damn her. She knew that by personalizing the vague entity she shielded that he'd be inhuman not to react.

"A daughter?"

Against his will, his voice softened, and he found himself examining her belly closer. He impatiently brushed aside her cupped hands and then snatched his own hand back when her belly rippled and jumped beneath his fingers.

"*Theos!* Is that her?"

Jewel smiled and nodded. "She's active this morning."

Piers shook his head in an attempt to brush away the spell. A daughter. Suddenly he envisioned a tiny little girl, a replica of Jewel but with his dark eyes. Damn her for making him dream again.

His expression hardened, and he once again focused his attention on Jewel. "Is she mine?"

Jewel met his steady gaze and nodded.

He swore softly. "We used protection. *I* used protection."

She shrugged. "She's yours."

"You expect me to accept that? Just like that?"

She struggled to sit up against her pillows, her fingers clenched into tight balls at her sides. "I haven't slept with another man in two years. She's yours."

He wasn't the gullible fool he'd been so many years ago. "Then you won't object to paternity testing."

She closed her eyes wearily and sank back into the covers. Hurt flickered in her eyes when she reopened them, but she shook her head. "No, Piers. I have nothing to hide."

"What is wrong with you? Why are you here in the hospital?" he asked, finally coming around to the matter at hand. He'd been completely blindsided by the discovery that the child she was pregnant with was…could be his.

"I've been ill," she said in a tired voice. "Elevated blood pressure. Fatigue. My doctor said my job had a lot to do with it, and he wants me to quit. He says I *must* quit, that I don't have a choice."

"What the devil have you been doing?" he demanded.

She lifted one shoulder. "Waitressing. It was all I could find on such short notice. I needed the money before I could move somewhere else. Somewhere warmer. Somewhere I could make more money. It's very expensive here in San Francisco."

"Then why did you come here from the island? You could have gone anywhere."

She cast him a bitter glance. "I have an apartment here. One that is paid for. After I was fired, I had little choice in where to go. I had to have a place to sleep. I intended to save enough money and then go somewhere else."

He flinched as guilt consumed him. Damn, but this was a mess. Not only had he had her fired, but he'd sent a pregnant woman into a bad situation.

"Look, Jewel, about your firing…"

She held up a hand, her expression fierce. "I don't want to discuss it. You're a coward and a bastard of the first order. I wouldn't have *ever* spoken to you again if our daughter didn't need you, if *I* didn't need your help."

"That's just it. I never intended for you to be fired," he said patiently.

She glared at him. "That's hardly comforting given that I *was* fired and that I *was* escorted out of your hotel."

He sighed. Now wasn't the time to try and reason with her. She was growing more upset by the minute. If she chose to believe the worst in him, and it was obvious she did, he was hardly going to change five months worth of anger and resentment in five minutes.

"So what is it that you need from me?" he asked. "I'll help in any way I can."

She stared at him, suspicion burning brightly in her ocean eyes. Maybe he was wrong to want his daughter to have his eyes. No, she should definitely have Jewel's eyes. Dark-haired like him, but with her mother's sea-green eyes. Or were they blue? He could never tell from one moment to the next.

Then her shoulders sank, and she closed her eyes. "My physician won't discharge me until he's certain I have someone to care for me."

She said the latter with a measure of distaste, as if it pained her to be dependent on anyone.

"I'll be on bed rest until my surgery."

Piers sat forward. "Surgery? Why do you need surgery? I thought you said you were only ill. Blood pressure." He knew enough about that from his sister-in-law's pregnancy to know that the prescribed treatment for stress or elevated blood pressure was merely rest and to be off one's feet. "You can't have surgery while you're pregnant. What about the baby?"

She stared back at him patiently. "That's just it. When they did a sonogram to check on the baby, they found a large cyst on one of my ovaries. Instead of shrinking, as a lot of cysts do during the course of the pregnancy, this one has gotten larger, and now it's pressing on the uterus. They have no choice but to remove it so that it won't interfere with the pregnancy or possibly even harm the baby."

Piers cursed. "This operation, is it dangerous? Will it harm the baby?"

"The doctor doesn't think so, but it has to be done soon."

He cursed again, though he didn't allow the words past his lips. He didn't want to be ensnared in another situation where he stood to lose everything. Once a fool, but never again. This time things would be done on his terms.

"You're going to marry me," he announced baldly.

Five

"You're out of your mind," Jewel burst out.

Piers's eyes narrowed. "I'd hardly say my speaking of marriage constitutes an unsound mind."

"Crazy. Certifiable."

He bristled and let out an irritated growl. "I am not crazy."

"You're serious!"

She stared at him with a mixture of stupefaction and horror.

His breath escaped in a long sound of exasperation.

Her mouth fell open. "For the love of God. You think I'd *marry* you?"

"There's no reason to sound so appalled."

"Appalled," she muttered. "That about covers my reaction. Look, Piers. I need your help. Your support. But I don't need marriage. Not to you. Never to you."

"Well if you want my support, you're damn well going to have to marry me for it," he growled.

"Get out," she bit off. She held a trembling hand up to point to the door, but Piers caught it and curled his fingers around hers. He brought it to the edge of the bed and gently stroked the inside of her wrist.

"I shouldn't have said that. You made me angry. If you're pregnant with my child, of course you'll have my support, Jewel. I'll do everything I can to provide for you and our daughter."

Astounded by his abrupt turnaround, she could only stare at him, her tongue flapping to try and come up with something, anything to say. How could he still affect her this way after all he'd done?

"Then you'll say no more about marriage?"

His lips tightened. "I didn't promise that. I have every intention of marrying you as quickly as possible and definitely before this surgery."

"But—"

He held up his hand, and to her utter annoyance, her mouth shut, cutting off her protest.

"You are having a dangerous surgery. You have no family, no one to be with you, to make decisions if the worst should happen."

A cold trickle of dread swept down her spine. How did he know anything about her family? Had he had her investigated? Her stomach rolled as nausea welled. She couldn't bear for anyone to know of her past. As far as she was concerned it didn't exist. She didn't exist.

"There has to be another way," she said faintly. Already the strain of him being here, of standing up against this hard man, was wearing on her.

It must have been obvious, because his expression

softened noticeably. "I'm not here to fight with you. We have a lot to work out and not much time. I need to speak with your doctor and have you transferred to a better facility. I'll want a specialist to take over your care. He can give us a second opinion on whether this surgery is the best solution with you pregnant. I'll see to the arrangements for our wedding."

"Stop right there," she said as fury worked its way up her spine until her neck was stiff and locked. "You won't come barging in here, taking over my life and making decisions for me. I'm not some brainless idiot who needs you to rush in and save the day. I've spoken to the doctors. I'm well aware of what needs to be done, and I will make the decision as to what is best for me and my daughter. If that bothers you, then you can take yourself right back to your island and leave me the hell alone."

He held up a placating hand. "Don't upset yourself, Jewel. I'm sorry if I've offended you. Taking over is what I do. You asked for my help, and I'm here to offer it, and yet now you don't seem to want it."

"I want your help without conditions."

For a long moment they stared at each other, neither backing down as the challenge was laid.

"And I'm afraid that I'm unwilling to just sit back and not have a say."

"You're not even convinced this is your child," she threw out.

He nodded. "That's true. I'd be a fool to blindly accept your word. We hardly know each other. How do I know you didn't set the entire thing up? Regardless, I'm willing to help. I have much to make up for. For now I'm willing to go with the assumption that you're carrying my daughter. I want us to marry before you have any further medical treatment."

"But that's just insane," she protested.

He continued on as if she hadn't spoken. "I'll have an agreement drawn up to protect both our interests. If it turns out you've lied and the child is not mine, the marriage will immediately be terminated. I'll provide a settlement for you and your daughter, and we'll go our separate ways."

She didn't miss the way he said "your daughter," the way he purposely distanced himself from the equation. If she lied. She almost shook her head. She would have had to have jumped directly from his bed into another man's for the timing to be such that the baby could be someone else's. What he must think of her. Hardly a basis for marriage.

"And if she is yours?" she asked softly.

"Then we remain married."

She was already shaking her head. "No. I don't want to marry you. You can't want this either."

"I won't argue about this, Jewel. You will marry me and you'll do it immediately. Think about what's best for your daughter. The longer we spend arguing, the longer you and the baby are at risk."

"You really are blackmailing me," she said in disbelief.

"Think what you want," he offered with a casual shrug.

"She is your child," she said fiercely. "You get those damn tests done, but she's yours."

Piers nodded. "I'm willing to concede that she could be mine. I wouldn't have offered marriage if I didn't think the possibility existed."

"And yet you don't want to wait for those results before you tie us together?"

"How strangely you put it," he said with mild amusement. "Our agreement will allow for any possibility. As

I've said, if it turns out you've lied to me, our marriage will end immediately. I'm prepared to be generous in spite of the lie, but it will be on my terms. And if, as you said, that she is my daughter, then the best course is for us to be married and provide a stable home for her."

"With two parents who can barely tolerate one another."

He raised one eyebrow. "I wouldn't go that far. I'd say we got on quite well together that night in my hotel room."

A deep flush worked its way over her cheeks. "Lust is no substitute for love, trust and commitment."

"And who is to say those things won't follow?"

She stared at him in astonishment.

"Give it a chance, Jewel. Who is to say what the future holds for us. For now, it isn't wise to dwell on things that might not even be an issue. We have your surgery to contend with and of course the results of the paternity test."

"Of course. Silly me to consider the cornerstones of marriage when in fact we're considering getting married."

"There is no need to be so sarcastic. Now, if we're finished, I suggest you get some rest. There are many things to be done, and the sooner I arrange everything, the sooner you can be at ease."

"I haven't said I'll marry you," she said evenly.

"No, and I'm waiting for your answer."

Frustration beat at her temples. How infuriating was this man. Arrogant. Convinced of getting his way each and every time. And yet, the jerk was right on all counts. She needed him. Their daughter needed him.

Sadness crept over her, and she lay back, closing her eyes. She felt disgustingly weepy. This was so far removed from the way she'd dreamed things might be one day. In her more sane moments, she'd accepted the fact that she'd probably never marry, never have someone she could absolutely trust. Trust just wasn't in her makeup. And yet, it hadn't stopped her fanciful daydreams of a strong, loving man. Someone who wouldn't abuse her trust. Someone who would love her unconditionally.

"It won't be as bad as that," Piers said gently as he took her hand in his once more.

She opened her eyes to see him staring intently at her.

"All right, Piers. I'll marry you," she said wearily. "But I'll have conditions of my own."

"I'll provide a lawyer to represent your interests. He can look over my part of the agreement and advise you accordingly."

How sterile and cold it all sounded. More like a hostile business takeover than a marriage. A delicate shiver skirted up her spine and prickled her nape. There was no doubt that she was making a mistake. Perhaps the biggest mistake of her life. But for her child, she'd do this. She'd do anything. From the moment she discovered she was pregnant, her child became everything to her. She wouldn't lose her daughter. If she had to marry the devil himself, she'd grit her teeth and bear it.

"How about I choose the lawyer and have him bill you," she offered sweetly.

To her surprise he chuckled. "Don't trust me? I suppose you have no reason to. Of course. Choose your lawyer and have him send me the bill."

Her eyes narrowed. He was positively magnanimous, but then he could afford to be now that he'd won.

"Is there anything you need? Anything you'd like me to bring you?"

She hesitated for a moment. "Food."

"Food? They don't feed you here?"

"Really good food," she said hopefully. "I'm starving."

He smiled, and she felt the jolt all the way to her toes. Damn the man for looking so disgustingly appealing. She didn't want to be attracted to him anymore. Her hand smoothed over her belly in another silent apology. She didn't regret a single thing about their night of passion, but it didn't mean she wanted to dwell on it forever.

"I will see what I can do about getting you some really good food. Now, get some rest. I'll be back after a while."

As if she would rest now that he'd arrived and turned her life upside down.

Then he surprised her by leaning down and brushing his lips across her forehead in a surprisingly tender gesture. She held her breath, enjoying the brief contact. As he drew away, his fingers trailed down her cheek.

"I don't want you to worry about anything. Just rest and get well and take good care of your…our daughter."

He seemed to struggle with the last as if he was making a concession to her claim, and yet, he looked grim. Maybe he had no wish for children. Tough. He now had a daughter, and he might as well get used to the idea.

He gave her one last look and then turned to walk briskly from the hospital room. When the door shut behind him, Jewel let out her breath in a long whoosh.

Married.

She couldn't imagine being married to such a hard man. She'd had enough hard people in her life. Emotionless, cold individuals with no heart, no love. And now she was con-signed to a marriage that would be a replica of her childhood.

Her hands rubbed and massaged her swollen belly. "It will never be like that for you, sweetie. I love you so much already, and there'll never be a day you won't know it. I swear. No matter what happens with your daddy, you'll always have me."

Six

"I've done a terrible thing," Piers said when his brother, Chrysander, muttered an unintelligible greeting in Greek.

Chrysander sighed, and Piers could hear him sit up in bed and fight the covers for a moment.

"Why is it becoming commonplace for my younger brothers to call me in the middle of the night with those exact words?"

"Theron messed up lately?" Piers asked in amusement.

"Not since he seduced a woman under his protection," Chrysander said dryly.

"Ahh, you mean Bella. Why do I imagine that it was she who did the seducing?"

"You're straying from the topic. What is this terrible thing you've done, and how much is it going to cost?"

"Maybe nothing. Maybe everything," Piers said quietly.

A curse escaped Chrysander's lips, and then Piers heard him say something to Marley in the background.

"Don't worry Marley over this," Piers said. "I'm sorry to have disturbed her sleep."

"It's too late for that," Chrysander growled. "Just give me a moment to go into my office."

Piers waited, drumming his fingers on the desk in his hotel room. Finally Chrysander came back on the line.

"Now tell me what's wrong."

Just like Chrysander to get to the point.

"I had an affair—a brief affair, a one-night stand really."

"So?" Chrysander asked impatiently. "This isn't new for you."

"She was my new assistant."

Chrysander cursed again.

"I didn't know she was my assistant until she showed up for work. I had her fired."

Chrysander groaned. "How much is she suing us for?"

"Let me finish." This time it was Piers who was impatient. "I didn't intend to fire her at all. I asked my human resources manager to transfer her, or promote her or pay her for her entire contracted term, but he only heard the get rid of her part and fired her. She disappeared before I could remedy the situation, and I wasn't able to locate her. Until now."

"Okay, so what's the problem?"

"She's in the hospital. She's ill, she needs a surgery…and she's pregnant."

Dead silence greeted his announcement.

"*Theos,*" Chrysander breathed. "Piers, you can't let this happen again. Last time—"

"I know," Piers said irritably. The last thing he needed was a recap of that disaster from his brother. It was bad enough he'd been made a complete fool of, but his brothers had witnessed the entire debacle.

"Are you certain the child is yours?"

"No. I've asked for paternity testing."

"Good."

"There's something else you should know," Piers said. "I'm going to marry her. Soon, as in the next few days."

"What? Have you lost your mind?"

"Funny, that's what she asked me."

"I'm glad one of you has sense then," Chrysander said heatedly. "Why on earth would you marry this woman when you don't even know if the child is yours?"

"It's amazing how the tables have turned," Piers said mildly.

"Don't even start. I heard the same thing from Theron when he was so set on marrying Alannis. Never mind that I was right about what a disaster that would be. You two warning me about Marley was an entirely different situation, and you know it. You don't have a relationship with this woman. You slept with her one night, and now she claims to be pregnant with your child, and you're going to marry her? Just like that?"

"She needs my help. I'm not stupid. I'm having our lawyer draw up an ironclad agreement that provides stipulations for the possibility that the child isn't mine. For now, with her surgery looming, it's best that we marry. This way I can make decisions for her care and that of the child's. If it does turn out to be my daughter, how would I feel if I had sat back and done nothing while I waited for the proof?"

"Daughter?"

"Yes. Apparently Jewel is pregnant with a girl."

Despite his doubts and his heavy suspicions, he couldn't help but smile at the image of a little girl with big eyes and a sweet smile.

"Jewel. What's her last name?"

"Oh no you don't, big brother. There's no need to get all protective and have her background dug up. I can handle this myself. You just concern yourself with your wife and my nephew."

"I don't want you hurt again," Chrysander said quietly.

And there it was. No matter how much he wanted to avoid the past, it was always there, hanging like a dark cloud. Unbidden, the image of another child, a sweet baby boy, dark-haired with a cherubic smile and chubby little legs, came painfully to mind. Eric. Not many days had gone by that Piers hadn't thought of him in some form or fashion, but not until now had such pain accompanied the memories.

"This time, I'm going to make sure that my interests are better protected," Piers said coldly. "I was a fool then."

Chrysander sighed. "You were young, Piers."

"It was no excuse."

"Call me if you need me. Marley and I would like to come to your wedding. It will be better if family is there."

"There's no need."

"There is every need," Chrysander said, interrupting him. "Let me know the details, and we'll fly out."

Piers's hand gripped the phone tighter. It was nice to have such unconditional support. And then he realized the irony. He hadn't exactly offered Jewel his unconditional support. He'd strong-armed her and taken advantage of her situation.

"All right. I'll call when I have the arrangements made."

"Be sure and let Theron know as well. He and Bella will want to be there."

Piers sighed. "Yes big brother."

Chrysander chuckled. "This is a small thing I ask. It's not as if you've ever listened to me before."

"Give Marley my love."

"I will—and Piers? Be careful. I don't like the sound of this at all."

Piers hung up the phone. He should call Theron, but he couldn't bring himself to face another inquisition. Especially now that Theron had joined the ranks of the deliriously happy. He'd be appalled that Piers was going to marry a woman he barely knew, a woman who might well be lying to him.

Instead he phoned his lawyer and outlined his situation. Then he arranged a security detail for Jewel. He and his brothers took no chances with those close to them after what had happened to Chrysander's wife, Marley. Next he called to see when Jewel's doctor would next be making his rounds. He intended to be there so he'd know exactly what was going on.

Lastly, he called a local restaurant and arranged for a full-course dinner to be prepared for pickup in an hour.

Jewel was ready to fidget right out of the bed. She'd only gotten up to use the bathroom, and now she'd decided she'd had enough. The doctor was releasing her tomorrow now that someone had shown up to take *care* of her. She had to work to keep the snort of derision from rising in her throat.

She could do without Piers Anetakis's brand of caring.

The thin hospital gown offered little in the way of modesty, and so after showering, she dressed in a pair of loose-fitting sweats and a maternity shirt. She toweled her hair as dry as she could and left it loose so it would finish drying.

She had settled in the small recliner to the side of her bed when the door opened, and Piers strode in carrying two large take-out bags.

She sat forward nervously as his gaze swept over her. Then his eyes narrowed, and he set the bags down on the bed.

"You should not have showered until I was here."

Her mouth fell open in shock. "What?"

"You could have fallen. You should have waited for me to help or at least called for the nurse."

"How do you know I didn't call for one of the nurses?"

He stared inquisitively at her, his eyes mocking. "Did you?"

"It's none of your business," she muttered.

"If you're pregnant with my child, it's every bit of my business."

"Look Piers, we need to get something straight right now. Me being pregnant with your child does not give you any rights over me whatsoever. I won't allow you to waltz in and take over my life."

Even as the sharp protest left her lips, she realized how stupid she sounded. That's precisely what he had done so far. Taken over. What else explained the reason for this marriage he proposed?

She bit her lip and looked away, her hand automatically moving to her belly in a soothing motion.

Piers began taking food out of the bags as if she'd said nothing at all. The smells wafted through her nostrils, and her stomach growled. Heavenly.

She raised an eyebrow. She wouldn't have thought he'd give much thought to what she could or couldn't have.

"Thank you, I'm starving."

He prepared a plate and handed it to her along with utensils. Then he fixed a plate for himself and settled on the edge of the bed.

"I can get back into the bed so you have a place to sit," she offered.

He shook his head. "You look comfortable. I'm fine."

They ate in silence, though she knew he watched her. She refused to acknowledge his perusal, though, and concentrated on the delicious food instead.

When she couldn't eat another bite, she sighed and put down her fork.

"That was wonderful, thank you."

He took the plate and set it on the counter along the wall. "Would you like to get back into bed now?"

She shook her head. "I've had enough bed to last a lifetime."

"But shouldn't you be in bed with your feet up?" he persisted.

"I'm doing well. The doctor wants me on moderated bed rest until my surgery. That means I can get up and move around. He just doesn't want me on my feet for long periods of time."

"And this job you had, you were on your feet all the time?" he asked with a frown.

"I was waitressing. It was necessary."

"You should have phoned me the minute you knew you were pregnant," he said fiercely.

Her expression turned murderous. "You had me fired. You told me quite plainly that you wanted nothing further to do with me. Why on earth would I be calling you? I wouldn't have called you now if I hadn't needed you so badly."

"Then I suppose I'll have to be grateful you needed me."

"I don't need you," she amended. "Our daughter does."

"You need me, Jewel. I have a lot to make up for, and I plan to do just that. We can talk about your firing when you aren't in the hospital and you're feeling better."

"About that," she began.

He raised an eyebrow. "Yes?"

"The doctor is releasing me in the morning."

"Yes, I know. I spoke to him before I came back to your room."

Her fingers curled into tight fists, but she kept the frustration from her expression. Or at least she tried.

"I don't need you hovering over me at every moment. You can drop me off at my apartment—"

Before she got any further he shook his head resolutely, his expression implacable.

"I've arranged for the rental of a house until your surgery. I'll take you there of course. I've hired a nurse to see to your needs—"

It was her turn to break in, her head shaking so stiffly that her neck hurt.

"No. Absolutely not. I won't have some nurse hired to babysit me. It's ridiculous. I'm not an invalid. I have to stay off my feet. Fine, I can do that without a nurse."

"Why must you be so difficult?" he asked mildly. "I'm only doing what is best for your health."

"If you want to hire someone, hire a cook," she muttered. "I'm terrible at it."

Amusement curved his hard mouth into a smile. It was amazing what a difference it made in his face. He looked almost boyish. She stared at him in astonishment.

"A cook can be arranged. I, of course, wish to see that my daughter and her mother are well fed. Does this mean you aren't going to fight moving in with me?"

She made a sound of protest, but it quickly died. She'd walked right into that one. With a long suffering sigh, she uttered a simple, "No."

"See, that wasn't so hard, now was it?"

"You can quit the gloating. It's not very attractive on you."

His grin broadened. The amazing thing was, it made him look quite charming. *Dangerous, Jewel. He's dangerous. Don't fall for that charm.*

"I'm going to take you home with me, Jewel," he said patiently. "There's little point in arguing. All the arrangements have been made. Tomorrow I hope to see to the wedding arrangements. Understandably, concerns for your health came before our marriage, but once I have you settled in, I'll see to the necessary plans."

The beginnings of a headache thrummed at her temples. Was this what her life was going to be like? Him calling all the shots and her meekly following along? Not if she could help it. Right now, she was tired, worried and more than a little stressed, and as weak as it made her feel to hand everything over to him, it also felt good to relinquish her problems. Even if it was just for a little while.

"Does your head hurt you?" he asked.

She drew her hand away, unaware until now that she'd been rubbing her forehead. "Stress," she said in a shaky voice. "It's been a long couple of weeks. I'm tired."

What an idiot she was, outlining her weaknesses in stark detail. As if he hadn't already honed in on her disadvantages.

To her surprise, he didn't make any sharp or sarcastic remarks. He took her hands gently in his, and lowered them to her lap. Then he carefully helped her up.

Too stunned to do more than gape at him, she cooperated without complaint. He stepped behind her and sank down onto the seat, pulling her down onto his lap.

She landed with a jolt of awareness that five long months hadn't diminished in the least. There was still potent chemistry between them, much to her dismay.

His warmth wrapped around her, soothing her despite her rioting emotions. She was almost in complete panic when his fingers dug into her hair and began massaging her scalp.

A soft moan of surrender escaped her. Bliss. Sheer, unadulterated bliss. His strong fingers worked to her forehead and then her temples.

Bonelessly she melted further into his chest. He stiffened slightly and then relaxed as he continued his ministrations. For several long minutes, neither spoke, and only the sound of her soft breathing could be heard.

"Better?" he asked softly.

She nodded, unable to form coherent words. She was floating on a cloud of sheer delight.

"You are worrying yourself too much, *yineka mou*. The stress is not good for you or the baby. Everything will be all right. You have my word on it."

The statement was intended to comfort her, and she did appreciate his effort. But for some reason, his vow sounded ominous to her ears. Almost like this was a turning point in her life where nothing would ever be the same. Like she was giving up control, not just for the short term.

Of course things are changing irrevocably, you idiot. You're pregnant and getting married. How much more change could you possibly make?

Still, she tried to draw some comfort in the serious promise in his voice. He didn't trust her. She didn't think he even particularly liked her, but he desired her, that much was obvious. And she desired him. It wasn't enough. Not even close, but it was all they had.

Not exactly a prime start to a marriage.

Seven

Jewel tilted her head so she could see out the window as Piers pulled through the gates of a sprawling estate covered in lush green landscaping and well manicured shrubbery. The house came into view when they topped the hill, and her eyes widened in appreciation. Despite the size of the grounds, the house was what she'd deem modest in comparison.

Still it was gorgeous. Two stories with dormers and ivy clinging to the front. He'd said he rented the place. Who knew such places were for rent?

He parked in front of the garage that was adjacent to the main house. Behind them, the car carrying her newly assigned security detail pulled in. Before she could get out, one of the guards appeared and opened her door. He hovered protectively, shielding her…from what? Only when Piers reached for her hand, did the guard step away.

"I'm not helpless, you know," she said dryly when he tucked her against his side. But she would have been lying if she denied that having his help thrilled her in an inexplicable way. His body was warm and solid against hers. Strong. The idea that she wasn't alone nearly brought her to her knees.

"I know this," he said in his brusque accent. "But you've only just gotten out of the hospital, and you're carrying a child. If at any time you need help, it is certainly now."

She relaxed against him, refusing to spoil their first moments home with senseless, petty arguments.

Home. The word struck her in the chest, and even as she thought it, she shook her head in mute denial. She had no home.

"Is there something wrong?" he asked as they stopped at the door.

Embarrassed over her emotional display, she uttered a low denial.

He opened the door, and they stepped into the expansive foyer. Beyond was an elegant double staircase curving toward the top where a hallway connected the two sides of the house.

"Come into the living room, and I'll see to your things."

She allowed him to lead her to a comfortable leather couch that afforded a view of the patio through triple French doors. It would be a perfect breakfast spot, she thought with longing. The morning sun would shine perfectly on the garden table.

What would it be like to have a home like this? Filled with laughter and children. And then it occurred to her that it was entirely possible that part of that dream would come true.

She looked down at the gentle mound covered by her

thin shirt and slowly smoothed her hand over it. The baby kicked, and Jewel smiled.

She wanted to give her daughter all the things she'd never had, the things she longed for. Love, acceptance. A stable home.

Would Piers provide those things? Everything but love. Could Jewel love her baby enough to compensate for a father who didn't want her or her mother?

Damn if she hadn't done what she'd sworn never to do.

Piers traipsed inside the living room, hauling her two suitcases with him.

"I'll take these upstairs, and then I'll be down to make us some lunch. Is there anything you need in the meantime?"

Unnerved by his consideration, she shook her head. "I'm fine."

"Good, then I'll be right back."

She heard him rattle up the stairs, and she returned her perusal moodily to the outside. No longer content to look from afar, she got up and walked to the glass doors. She pressed her hand to the panes as she gazed over the magnificently rendered gardens.

It was extremely beautiful, but it almost looked sterile, as if no one ever touched it, or even breathed on it for that matter. It seemed…artificial. Not a living, breathing entity. Not like the ocean. It was always alive, rolling, sometimes peaceful and serene and at other times angry and forbidding.

A hand slipped over her shoulder, and she jumped. As she turned, she saw that Piers stood behind her, his expression mild and unthreatening.

"Sorry if I startled you. I called from across the room, but you didn't hear me obviously."

She offered a half smile, suddenly nervous in his presence.

"It's beautiful isn't it?"

"Yes, it is," she agreed. "I prefer the ocean, though. It's more…untamed."

"You find these gardens tame?"

"Mmm-hmm."

"I suppose I can see your point. Would you like to eat now? I had something dropped by before we arrived. It will only take a few minutes to warm everything up."

She turned sideways to face him. "Could we eat outside? It's a beautiful day."

"If you wish. Why don't you go on outside. I'll bring out the food in a moment."

His footsteps retreated across the wooden floors. When he was gone, she slipped out of the French doors and onto the stone patio.

The coolness caused her to shiver, but it was a beautiful day, one of the few where nothing marred the blue sky, and she didn't want to waste it by returning indoors.

She settled into one of the chairs to wait for Piers. It seemed odd to have this arrogant man waiting on her. He was clearly used to having the tables turned and being served.

The doors opened, and Piers elbowed his way out carrying two trays. He was a man of continuing surprises. He'd shown up at the hospital in time for her release, wearing a pair of faded jeans and a casual polo shirt, a far cry from the expensive designer clothing she knew he usually wore. He looked almost approachable. No less desirable, but definitely less threatening. In a more cynical moment, she wondered if he'd done it on purpose to lull her into a false sense of security.

He set a tray in front of her then placed his own across the table before taking a seat. She picked up her fork but made the mistake of looking over at him before she began to eat. He was staring intently at her, his food untouched.

"We have a lot to talk about, Jewel. After you eat, I plan to have the conversation we should have had a long time ago."

He sounded ominous, and a prickle of unease swept over her. What was left for them to discuss? He'd demanded she marry him, and she'd agreed. He'd demanded she move in with him, and she'd agreed. Quite frankly her acquiescence was starting to irritate the hell out of her.

They ate in silence, though she knew he watched her. The heat of his stare blazed over her skin, but she refused to acknowledge his perusal. He already had enough power over her.

When she'd finished, she put her fork down, and still refusing to look at him, she turned her gaze back to the gardens.

"Ignoring me won't help."

Finally she turned, sure she must look guilty. Now she felt childish for being so obvious, but the man made her nervous.

"We need to clear the air on a few matters. Mainly your firing."

She stiffened and clenched her fingers into small fists. "I'd just as soon not discuss it. No good can come of it, and I *am* supposed to keep my stress level down."

"I never intended to have you fired, Jewel. It was a despicable thing to have happened to you, and I accept full blame."

"Well who the hell else's fault would it be?" she demanded.

"It wasn't what I intended," he said again.

"Whether you intended it or not, it's what happened. Mighty coincidental that I got the sack as soon as you found out who I was, wouldn't you say?"

Piers blew out his breath, and his gaze narrowed. "You aren't going to make this easy, are you?"

She leaned back, this time giving him the full intensity of her stare. "Why should it be easy for you? It wasn't easy for me. I had no money left, no job. I came here because it was the only place I had to stay, and waitressing was the only quick job I could land. Then I started getting sick." She stopped and shook her head. She wasn't going to get into it with him.

"You're right. I'm sorry."

He looked and sounded sincere. Enough so that her next question slipped out before she could think better of it.

"If I wasn't supposed to be fired, how exactly did I end up sacked and escorted out of the hotel?"

Piers winced and dragged a hand through his hair. "As I said, it's completely my fault. I told my human resources manager to reassign you, or promote you or even to pay you for the term of your contract but I'm afraid the first words out of my mouth were to get rid of you. The rest, unfortunately, he didn't hear because the connection was severed. By the time I returned to the hotel and discovered the misunderstanding, you were gone. I had no luck tracing your whereabouts. In fact, I'd given up ever hearing from you again until you called."

She stared at him in disbelief. First, she couldn't believe he'd actually admitted his wrongdoing. Second, she couldn't fathom him looking for her afterward. It sounded suspiciously like he genuinely regretted what had happened.

"I don't get it," she said with genuine confusion. "Why couldn't we have just been adults about it? Why was it so important to you to get rid of me? I realize it wasn't an ideal situation, but it was an honest mistake. Neither of us knew who the other was or God knows I wouldn't have gone to bed with you that night."

"Then I guess it's a good thing you didn't know who I was," he said softly.

She looked down at her belly. "Yes, I don't regret it now at all."

"Did you then?"

He didn't look offended, only genuinely curious. He'd been honest with her so far, so she couldn't be anything other than completely honest with him.

"No. I didn't regret our night together."

He seemed satisfied with her answer. "To answer your question, it wasn't personal. What I mean is that it's not as if it was something you did. I have a strict policy about allowing anyone to work closely with me who has had any sort of a personal relationship with me. It's a necessary rule, unfortunately."

She raised an eyebrow. "You say that as if you were once burned."

"In a manner of speaking. My brother's personal assistant was enamored with him, but she was also selling company secrets and framed my sister-in-law."

"Sounds like a soap opera," Jewel muttered.

He chuckled. "It seemed like one at the time."

"You could have simply told me. You owed me that much given the fact we had spent the night together," she said, pinning him with the force of her gaze. "If you'd been up front with me, none of this would have happened. There would have been no misunderstanding."

"You're right. I'm afraid the shock of finding out who you were made my judgment particularly bad. I'm sorry."

His quietly spoken apology softened some of her anger. If she was honest, she still held resentment for the easy way he'd summarily dismissed her from his life. Not that she'd expected undying love and commitment, but hadn't the night meant something? Even enough to rate a personal dismissal instead of the job being handed off to a stooge?

Still, if this marriage was to be anything short of difficult and laced with animosity, she knew he had to let go of some of that resentment. Be the bigger person and all that jazz. Funny how taking the high road was never particularly fun.

"I accept your apology."

Surprise flickered in his dark eyes. "Do you really, I wonder?"

"I didn't say you were my best friend," she said dryly. "Merely that I'd accepted your apology. It seems the thing to do in light of our impending nuptials."

Amusement replaced the surprise. "I have a feeling we're going to get along just fine together, *yineka mou.*" His gaze dropped to her stomach. "That is if you're telling me the truth."

For a moment, pain shadowed his eyes, and she wondered what sort of hell occurred in his past that would make him so distrustful. It went beyond mistrust. He didn't *want* to be the father of her child. He wanted her to be a liar and a deceiver. It was as if he knew how to handle those. But a woman telling him the truth? That was the aberration.

She must be insane to walk into this type of situation. There was every way for her to lose and no way to win.

"It does me little good to tell you that you're the father when you're determined not to believe me," she said evenly. "We'll have the paternity tests done and then you'll know."

"Yes. Indeed we'll know," he said softly.

"If you'll excuse me, I need to go dig out my laptop," she said as she rose from her seat. "I need to send an e-mail."

"And I have arrangements to make for our wedding."

She nodded because if she tried to say anything, she'd

choke. Not looking back at him, she hurried to the doors and went inside. Piers hadn't told her which bedroom was hers, but she'd find it easily enough.

She hit the stairs, and after going into three rooms on the upper level, she found her bags lying on the bed.

She unpacked her clothing first and put everything away before settling back onto the bed with her laptop. She checked her e-mail, but didn't see anything from Kirk. Not that she expected to. Sometimes they went months with no communication depending on his assignment and whether she was in a place she could e-mail him. Still, she felt like she owed him an explanation, and so she spilled the entire sordid tale in an e-mail that took her half an hour to compose.

When she was done, she was worn out and feeling more than a little foolish. There was no advice Kirk could offer, but she felt better for unloading some of her worries. He'd know better than anyone her fears of marriage and commitment.

Leaving her laptop open, she leaned back on the soft pillows to stare up at the ceiling. Contemplating her future had never been quite so terrifying as it was now.

Piers walked up the stairs toward Jewel's room. She'd been sequestered for two hours now. Surely that was enough time to have completed her personal business.

He stopped at her door and knocked softly, but he heard no answer from within. Concerned, he pushed open the door and stepped inside.

Jewel was curled on her side, her head buried in the down pillows. Sound asleep. She looked exhausted.

Her laptop was precariously close to the edge of the bed, and he hurried over to retrieve it before it fell. When he placed it on the dresser, the screen came back up and he saw that a new e-mail message was highlighted by the cursor. It was from someone named Kirk.

With a frown, he scrolled down the preview screen to read the short message.

Jewel,
I'm on my way home. Don't do anything until I get there. Okay? Just hang tight. I'll be there as soon as I can hop a flight.
Kirk

Piers stiffened. Hell would freeze over before he'd allow this man to interfere in his and Jewel's relationship. She'd agreed to marry him, and marry him she would. He didn't question why it was suddenly so important that the wedding take place, but he'd be damned if he let another man call the shots.

With no hesitation, he clicked on the delete button and then followed it to the trash bin to permanently delete it from her computer. Afterward, he pulled her e-mail back up and then replaced the laptop on her bed, making sure it was far enough from the edge so that it wouldn't topple over.

For a long moment, he stood by her bed and stared down at her sleeping face. Drawn to the pensive expression, even in rest, he touched a few strands of her blond hair, smoothing them from her cheek.

What demons existed in her life? She didn't trust him. Not that he blamed her, but it went beyond anger or a sense of betrayal. She wore shadows like most women wore make-up. Somewhere, some way, someone had hurt her badly. They had that in common.

As much as he'd like to swear never to hurt her and to

protect her from those who would, he knew that if she'd lied to him about the child, that he'd crush her without a second thought.

Eight

Jewel studied the unsmiling face of the man she'd chosen to represent her interests and wondered if any lawyer had a sense of humor or if they were all cold, calculating sharks.

But then she supposed when it came to her future and that of her child, she wanted the biggest, baddest shark in the ocean.

"The agreement is pretty straightforward, Miss Henley. It is in essence a prenuptial agreement which states that Mr. Anetakis's assets remain his in the event of a divorce and that yours remain yours."

Jewel snorted in amusement. What assets? She didn't have a damn thing, and Piers knew it.

"What else?" she asked impatiently. With a man like Piers, nothing could be as simple as it appeared. There were strings, hidden provisions. She just had to find them. "I want a complete explanation, line by line."

"Very well."

He shoved his glasses on and picked up the sheaf of papers as he took his seat again.

"Mr. Anetakis will provide a settlement for you regardless of the paternity of the child you carry. If DNA testing proves the child his, then he will retain custody of the child in the event of a divorce."

Her mouth fell open. "What?" She made a grab for the paper her lawyer held, scanning the document until she found the clause he referred to.

"He's out of his damn mind. There is no way in hell I'll sign anything that gives up custody of my child."

"I can strike the clause, but it's possible he won't agree."

She leaned forward, her breath hissing through her teeth. "I don't give a damn what he agrees to. I won't sign it unless this so-called clause is removed in its entirety."

Furious, she stood and snatched the paper back as the lawyer reached for it. "Never mind. I'll see to it myself."

She stormed out of the lawyer's office into the waiting room where Piers sat. He was sitting on the far side, his laptop open and his cell phone to his ear. When he looked up and saw her, he slowly closed the laptop.

"Is there a problem?"

"You bet there is," she said behind gritted teeth.

She thrust the offending piece of paper at him, pointing to the custody clause.

"If you think I'm signing anything that gives away custody of my child, you're an idiot. Over my dead body will I ever be separated from my child. As far as I'm concerned, you can take this…this prenuptial agreement and stick it where the sun doesn't shine."

He raised one dark eyebrow and stared back at her in silence.

"You don't seriously think that I would give up custody of *my* child, do you? If indeed it turns out I am the father."

She threw up her hands in exasperation. "You just don't miss a chance to take your potshots at me. I'm well aware of the fact that you don't believe this child is yours. Believe me, I get it. Reminding me at every opportunity just serves to further piss me off. And haven't you ever heard of a thing called joint custody? You know, that thing called compromise, where the parents consider what's best for the child and agree to give her equal time with her parents?"

"If the child is mine, I don't intend to see her on a part-time basis, nor do I intend I should have to work around your schedule. I can certainly provide more for her than you can. I'm sure she'd be much better off with me."

She curled her fingers into a tight fist, crumpling the document as rage surged through her veins like acid.

"You sanctimonious bastard. Where do you get off suggesting that my child would be better off with you? Because you have more money? Well big whoop. Money can't buy love, or security. It can't buy smiles or happiness. All the things a child needs most. Quite frankly, the fact that you think she would be so much better off with you tells me you don't have the first clue about children or love. How could you? I doubt you've ever loved anyone in your life."

Her chest heaved, and the paper was now a crumpled, soggy scrap in her hand. She started to hurl it at his feet, but he quickly rose and gripped her wrist, preventing her action. His eyes smoldered with rage, the first sign of real emotion she'd seen in him.

"You assume far too much," he said icily.

She wrenched her hand free and took a step backward.

"I won't sign it, Piers. As far as I'm concerned this marriage doesn't need to take place. There is no amount of desperation that would make me sign away my rights to my child."

He studied her for a long moment, his face as immovable as stone. "All right," he finally said. "I'll have my lawyer strike the clause. I'll call him now and he can courier over a new agreement."

"I'd wait," she said stiffly. "I'm not finished with my stipulations yet. I'll let you know when we're done."

She turned and stalked back into the lawyer's office, only to find him standing in the doorway, amusement carved on his face when she'd sworn he couldn't possibly have a sense of humor.

"What are you looking at?" she growled.

He sobered, although his eyes still had a suspicious gleam. "Shall we get on to your additions to the agreement?"

Three hours later, the final contract had been couriered from Piers's lawyer's office, and she and Piers read over and signed it together.

Jewel had insisted on an ironclad agreement that stated they would share custody of their child but that she was the primary custodian. She could tell Piers wasn't entirely happy with the wording, but she'd been resolute in her refusal to sign anything less.

"Clearly you've never learned the art of negotiation," Piers said dryly as they left the lawyer's office.

"Some things aren't negotiable. Some things *shouldn't* be negotiable. My child isn't a bargaining chip. She never will be," she said fiercely.

He held up his hands in mock surrender. "All I ask is that you see my side of the equation. As determined as you are to retain custody of your child, I am equally determined not to let go of mine."

Something in his expression caused her to soften, some of her anger fleeing and leaving her oddly deflated. For a moment, she could swear he seemed afraid and a little vulnerable.

"I do see your point," she said quietly. "But I won't apologize for reacting as I did. It was a sneaky, underhanded thing to do."

"I apologize then. It was not my intention to upset you so. I was simply seeking to keep my child where she belongs."

"Maybe what we should be doing is working to prevent a divorce in the first place," she said tightly. "If we manage to make this marriage a success as you have suggested, then we won't have to worry about custody battles."

He nodded and opened the car door for her. She settled in but he stood there for a long moment, his hand on the door. "You're right. The solution is to make sure it never comes down to a divorce."

He quietly closed her door and strode around to his side. He slid in beside her and started the engine.

"Now that the unpleasantness is out of the way, we should move on to the more enjoyable aspects of planning a wedding."

Thus began an afternoon of shopping that made her head spin. Their first stop was at a jeweler. When they were shown a tray of stunning diamond engagement rings, she made the mistake of asking the price. Piers clearly wasn't happy with her question, but the jeweler answered her with ease. It was all she could do to scrape her jaw off the floor.

She shook her head, putting her hands out as she backed away from the counter. Piers caught her around the waist and pulled her back with tender amusement.

"Don't disappoint me. As a woman it's supposed to be ingrained for you to want to pick the biggest, most expensive ring in the shop."

"Indeed," the shop owner said solemnly.

"It's not good form to ask the price anyway," Piers continued. "Just pick the one you want and pretend there are no price tags."

"Your fiancé is a very wise man," the man behind the counter said. Laughter shone in the merchant's eyes, and Jewel relaxed at their teasing.

Trying not to think about the fact that what one ring cost could feed an entire third world nation, she went about studying each setting. After trying on no less than a dozen, she found the perfect ring.

It was a simple pear-shaped diamond, flawless as far as her untrained eye could tell. On either side was a small cluster of tiny diamonds.

"Your lady has exquisite taste."

"Yes, she does. Is this the one you want, *yineka mou?*" Piers asked.

She nodded, ignoring the sick feeling in her stomach. "I don't want to know how much it cost."

Piers laughed. "If it will make you feel better, I'll match the cost of the ring with a donation to the charity of your choice."

"Now you're making fun of me."

"Not at all. It's nice to know my new wife won't break me inside of a year."

He was trying hard to keep from laughing, and she leveled a glare at him. She marveled at the ease in which he flipped his credit card to the cashier, as if he were paying for a drink instead of a ring that costs thousands upon thousands of dollars.

He slid the ring on her finger and curled her hand until it made a fist. "Leave it on. It's yours now."

She glanced down, unable to keep from admiring it. It *was* a gorgeous ring.

"Now that the ring is out of the way, we should move onto other things like a dress and any other clothing you might need."

"Wow, a man who likes to shop. However have you existed as a single man this long?" she teased.

His expression became shuttered, and she mentally sighed at having once again said the wrong thing at the wrong time.

Determined to salvage the rest of the day despite its rocky start, she tucked her hand into his arm as they left the jeweler.

"I'm starving. Can we eat before we attack the rest of the shopping?"

"Of course. What would you like to eat?"

"I'd love a big, nasty steak," she said wistfully.

He laughed. "Then by all means, let's go kill a cow or two."

Nine

The fact that Jewel hid in her room didn't make her a coward exactly. It just made her reserved and cautious. Downstairs, Piers greeted his family who had flown in for the wedding. She still couldn't understand why. It wasn't as if this was a festive occasion, the uniting of kindred souls and all that gunk that surrounded marriage ceremonies.

All she knew about the rest of the Anetakis clan was that Piers had two older brothers, and both were recently married, and at least one child had been added. Hers would be the second.

And from all Piers had told her, his brothers were disgustingly in love.

She closed her eyes in recognition that she was green with envy, and she dreaded having to meet these disgustingly happy people.

They'd know it wasn't all hearts and roses between her and Piers. For that matter, she was sure Piers had told them the entire truth and that they were marrying because of a one-night stand and a faulty condom.

She stared back at her reflection in the mirror and tried to erase the glum look from her face. The dress she'd chosen for the occasion was a simple white sheath with spaghetti straps. The material gathered gently at her breasts, molding to her shape then falling over her belly where it strained and then hung loose down her legs.

She'd debated on whether to put her hair up or leave it down, but Piers had seemed to delight in her hair the night they met and so in a moment of sheer vanity, she brushed it until it shone and let it hang over her shoulders.

And now she procrastinated like the coward she was, knowing everyone was downstairs waiting for her.

Still bereft of the courage needed to walk down those stairs, she walked to her window to look down over the gardens. The sky was overcast and light fog had descended over the grounds. A perfect fit to her melancholy mood.

For how long she stood, she wasn't sure. A warm hand slid over her bare shoulder, but she didn't turn. She knew it was Piers.

Then something cool slithered around her neck, and she did turn her head.

"Be still a moment," he said as he reached under her hair to fasten a necklace at her nape. "My wedding gift to you. There are earrings to match, but I honestly couldn't remember if your ears were pierced or not."

She put a hand to the necklace and then hastened to the mirror so she could see. A gasp of surprise escaped when she saw the exquisite diamond arrangement.

"Piers, it's too much."

He smiled over her shoulder. "My sisters-in-law inform me that a husband can never do too much for his wife."

She smiled back. "They sound like smart women."

"There, that wasn't so bad was it?"

Her brow crinkled. "What?"

"Smiling."

Her eyes flashed in guilty awareness. He held out the box with the earrings, and she gazed in wonder at the large stones twinkling back at her.

"Are your ears pierced?"

She nodded. "I seldom wear earrings, but they are pierced."

"Then I hope you'll wear these today."

She took them and quickly fastened them in her ears. When her gaze returned to his, she found him watching her intently.

"Speaking of my sisters-in-law, they're anxious to meet you."

"And not your brothers?" she asked.

"They are a bit more reserved in their welcome. They worry for me. I'm afraid it's a family tradition to try and ruin the nuptials of the others," he said dryly.

She didn't know whether to laugh or feel dismay. Finally laughter won out. "Well at least you're honest. For that I'm grateful. It will keep me from making a fool of myself in their presence."

He shrugged. "You have nothing to be reserved about. You are to be my wife and that fact affords you the respect you are due. Theron is the soft touch in the family anyway. You'll have him eating out of your hand in no time."

She couldn't imagine anyone related to Piers being a soft touch.

"Are you ready?" he asked as he slipped his hands over

her shoulders. He squeezed reassuringly as if sensing her deep unease. "We have just enough time for you to be introduced to my family before the minister is due to arrive for the ceremony."

Inhaling deeply, she nodded. He took her hand firmly in his and led her out of the bedroom and down the stairs. As they neared the bottom, she heard the murmur of voices in the living room.

Butterflies scuttled around her stomach, and the baby kicked, perhaps in protest of her mother's unease.

When they rounded the corner, Jewel took in the people assembled in the living room with a bit of awe. The two men were obviously Piers's brothers. There was remarkable resemblance. Both were tall and dark-haired, but their eyes were lighter than Piers's, a golden hue while Piers's were nearly black.

The two women standing next to his brothers were as different as night and day. Before she could continue her silent perusal, they looked up and saw her.

The brothers gave her guarded looks while the two women smiled welcomingly. She was grateful for that at least.

"Come, I'll introduce you," Piers murmured.

They closed the distance, stopping a few feet from the two couples.

"Jewel, this is my oldest brother Chrysander and his wife Marley. Their son, Dimitri is with his nanny for the day."

Jewel offered a tremulous smile. "I'm happy to meet you."

Marley smiled, her blue eyes twinkling with friendliness. "We're happy to meet you too, Jewel. Welcome to the family. I hope you'll be happy. When are you due?"

Jewel blinked and then returned her smile. "I'm a little over five months along."

"Hello, Jewel," Chrysander said in his deep voice.

She swallowed and nodded her greeting to Piers's oldest brother. Intimidating. How could anyone stand to be around the three of the Anetakis brothers at the same time?

Piers turned to the other couple. "This is my brother Theron and his wife, Bella." Piers's entire expression softened into a fond smile when he touched Bella's arm. She smiled mischievously back at Piers and then looked up at Jewel.

"We're both happy to meet you, Jewel," Bella said. She nudged Theron with her elbow. "Aren't we, Theron?"

"Of course, Bella *mou*," he said in a teasing tone. It was as if all attempt to maintain a serious air went out the window when he looked at his wife. Then he turned his attention to Jewel. "Welcome to our family. I'm not sure whether to offer my congratulations or my condolences on marrying my brother."

Jewel smiled at his attempt at humor, and Piers snorted.

"If you're quite through insulting me, I'll offer everyone a drink to celebrate the occasion. The minister should be here at any moment to perform the ceremony."

The others watched her curiously as Piers left her side to collect a chilled bottle of champagne. He passed glasses to everyone and then popped the cork.

When he came to her, he handed her a glass of mineral water instead. She was touched by his thoughtfulness and smiled her thanks.

Chrysander cleared his throat, and Marley slipped her arm into his. "Our best wishes for a long and…happy marriage," he added after a slight pause.

They raised their glasses in a toast, and for a moment, Jewel wished, oh how she wished that it was all real, and that this was her family and that she and Piers were in love and expecting their first child with all the joy of a happily married couple.

She dreamed of Christmas celebrations, birthdays and get-togethers just for the heck of it and a loud rambunctious family, loyal to a fault.

Tears pricked her eyelids as she bade goodbye to that dream and embraced her reality. She hastily gulped her water in an effort to regain control of her emotions.

Piers stood at her side and bent his head low to her ear. "What is it, *yineka mou?* What has upset you?"

"I'm fine," she said, pasting on a bright smile.

The doorbell rang, and she jumped.

His fingers cupped her elbow, and he rubbed a thumb across her skin in a soothing manner. "It's just the minister here to marry us. I'll go let him in."

She almost asked him not to go, but how silly was she to be worried about being left alone with his relatives? She chanced a glance at the two couples, standing so close, so lovingly together, and her heart ached all over again.

"Between you and Marley, Theron is going to get all the wrong ideas," Bella said to Jewel.

"And how is this?" Theron demanded.

"All these babies and pregnant women," she said mischievously. "I fully expect Theron to start hinting about knocking me up just any day now."

Jewel laughed, charmed by Bella's easy humor and how relaxed she was around everyone. Clearly she wasn't worried about her place in this family. No one seemed to mind her outrageous statement in the least.

Marley tried to stifle her laughter while Chrysander just groaned. Theron's eyes took on a sensual light that almost made Jewel feel like a voyeur.

"Oh no, Bella *mou*. We have much practicing to do before we get you pregnant."

"See, Jewel, it's not so hard to train the Anetakis men," she said cheekily. "Marley has whipped Chrysander into admirable shape, while I have turned Theron to my way of thinking. I can't imagine you being any less successful with Piers."

"Theron, keep your woman quiet," Chrysander said mildly. "She's inciting discontent among the female ranks."

Marley elbowed him sharply, but her eyes were alight with amusement and love.

Piers walked back in with an elderly man, their heads turned in conversation. When the minister saw Jewel, he smiled and went forward, his hands outstretched.

"You must be the bride to be. You look lovely, my dear. Are you ready for the ceremony to begin?"

She swallowed and nodded, though her legs were trembling.

The minister introduced himself to the others, and after a few moments of polite conversation, Piers motioned that he was ready to begin.

It was all quite awkward, at least for Jewel. The rest acted as if this was the sort of ceremony they attended every day. Piers and Jewel stood in front of the minister while each couple flanked them.

Her throat tightened as she listened to Piers promise to love, honor and cherish her all the days of his life and until death do they part. And then it struck her square in the face that she wanted him to love her. Why? Did that mean she loved him? No, she didn't. She couldn't. She didn't know how to love any more than she knew how to be loved. But it didn't stop the yearning inside.

When the ceremony concluded, Piers brushed a perfunctory kiss across her lips and then stepped back to receive his brothers' somewhat muted congratulations.

Chrysander insisted on taking them all out to eat afterward, and a limousine took all three couples into the heart of the city to an upscale restaurant that boasted delicious seafood.

She was hungry, but the idea that she was now married effectively put a damper on her appetite. She picked and pushed at her food until finally Piers took notice.

He picked up her hand, and the band he'd placed on her finger just hours before gleamed behind the diamond engagement ring in the low light.

"Are you ready to return home?" he whispered so the others wouldn't hear. "I can send them on at any time."

"They're your family," she protested. "I've no wish to cut short your visit."

He laughed. "You're very thoughtful, *yineka mou,* but I see them often, and if there is ever a time I can send them away, surely my wedding day is one of them? They would understand—having had their wedding nights not too long ago."

She froze as his meaning became clear. Surely he wasn't thinking that…no, he couldn't, could he? He'd been present when her doctor said there was no reason she couldn't indulge in lovemaking, but she'd assumed that Piers had taken it as the doctor thinking they were in a normal relationship. Did this mean he wanted to make love to her? To actually consummate the marriage?

His hand covered hers, idly stroking the tops of her fingers as he turned to the others and told them that he and Jewel were ready to go.

There were hugs, polite kisses and teasing good-byes.

Piers hugged each of his sisters-in-law, and she could tell that he regarded them with great affection. It was quite a change to the way he looked at her with so much distrust in those dark eyes.

And then they were on their way. Piers had left the limousine to the others and called for a car to pick them up. The ride home was quiet, and finally, unable to stand the tension, she turned her head in the darkness of the backseat only to see him staring at her, those dark eyes nearly invisible.

"What is bothering you, *yineka mou?*"

"Are you expecting a wedding night?" she blurted.

White teeth flashed as he smiled. It was a decidedly predatory smile, and it sent shivers down her spine.

"But of course. You're my wife now. A wedding night usually does follow a wedding, does it not?"

"I…I just wasn't sure, I mean this isn't a real marriage, and I didn't think you wanted much to do with me."

"Oh, I intend for it to be very real," he said softly. "Just as I intend for you to spend tonight and every night in my bed."

Ten

All she had to do was say no. It wasn't as if Piers would force her. Jewel stepped from the car, her hand in Piers's as he pulled her to his side. A shiver overtook her when the night chill brushed her skin, and she unconsciously moved closer to his warmth.

The question was, did she want to tell him no? And what purpose would it serve except to make him further distrust her and her motives?

As soon as the thought materialized, she clenched her teeth in anger. If the only reason she could muster to go to bed with him was so that he'd trust her more then she needed a serious reality check, not to mention she needed a few more brain cells.

Admit it, you want him.

And there it was. She did. The one night they'd shared burned brightly in her memory. She was married to him, and she wanted him to love her. She wanted him to trust her, and neither could happen if she maintained the distance between them.

Determined to embrace her marriage without being a martyr, she slipped her fingers tighter through Piers's and hurried alongside him into the house.

"I know today was hard for you, *yineka mou*. I hope it wasn't too taxing for you and the baby."

Had he changed his mind about making love to her? It sounded like he was offering an out. Or was he simply giving her the choice?

"I'm perfectly all right," she said softly as they stepped into the foyer.

He turned, putting his hands gently on her upper arms. "Are you?"

She stared back, knowing what he was really asking. Slowly she nodded, her senses firing in rapid succession.

"Be sure, Jewel. Be very sure."

Again she nodded, and before she could say or do anything else, he pulled her to him and covered her mouth hotly with his.

He swallowed her breath, took every bit of air and left her gasping for more. How was it he made her so weak? She sagged against him, clutching desperately at his shirt.

His tongue invaded her mouth, sliding sensuously over her lips and inside, tasting her and giving her his taste.

"Sweet," he murmured. "So sweet. I want you, *yineka mou*. Say you want me too. Let me take you upstairs. I want to make love to you again."

"Yes. Please, yes." She gasped when he swung her into his arms. "Piers no, I'm too heavy."

"Do you doubt my strength?" he asked in amusement as he mounted the stairs.

"I'm huge," she said in exasperation.

"You're beautiful."

He carried her through the doorway to the master bedroom and laid her carefully on the bed. With gentle fingers he slipped the thin straps over her shoulders and let them fall. He tugged farther until the dress eased over her sensitive breasts, the material scraping lightly at her nipples.

Farther and farther, it inched over her belly, then to her hips and finally down her legs. When it swirled around her ankles, he pulled it free and dropped it on the floor.

Sharp tingles raced up her legs when he rasped his palms back up to her hips where he tucked his thumbs underneath the lace of her panties. Then he lowered his mouth and pressed a kiss to her taut belly as he slid the underwear down and then free. Her legs parted in exquisite anticipation as his mouth traveled lower and lower still.

Cupping her behind, he gently spread her wider, and his tongue found her in a heated rush. She arched off the bed, twisting wildly as pleasure consumed her.

His mouth found her again and again, gentle and worshipping. It was hard to breathe, hard to think, hard to do anything but feel. Her orgasm built, and every muscle in her body tightened in response. Just when she knew she couldn't bear it any longer, he pulled away, and she whimpered in protest.

"Shhh." He murmured to her again in Greek, raining soft words over her skin as he moved up her body. How had he gotten his clothes off without her noticing?

Flesh against flesh, smooth, comforting, a balm to her reeling senses. His mouth closed around one taut nipple, sucking and tugging. One hand cupped her rounded middle, his fingers splayed possessively over their child.

It was the first movement he'd made to actually acknowledge her presence, and she wondered if he even knew what he was doing.

"Open your legs for me, *yineka mou.* Welcome me inside."

She could barely make herself respond. She shook and quivered as he settled between her thighs, his shaft nudging impatiently.

And then he was inside her in one smooth thrust.

She cried out and gripped his shoulders, her nails digging deep.

"That's it. Hold on to me. I've got you."

Their lips fused, their tongues tangling wildly as their bodies met and retreated. Pressure built until she simply couldn't bear it any longer. Her release exploded with the force of a hurricane.

He followed, surging into her, over and over, his husky groan filling her ears as he poured himself into her.

She closed her eyes, allowing sweet fuzzy bliss to encompass her, and when she gained awareness, it was to Piers's arms wrapped tightly around her, her body tucked into his side.

His lips moved through her hair as his hand went to cup her backside in a possessive gesture. She melted bonelessly into him and sighed in contentment. The wispy hairs on his chest tickled her nose and whispered across her lips, but she didn't move. She felt safe. More than that, she felt loved.

Jewel awoke the next morning to Piers sitting on the side of the bed holding a tray with breakfast and a single long-stemmed rose. He had only a pair of silk pajama bottoms on, and her gaze was drawn to his muscled chest, a chest she'd slept on for most of the night.

"Good morning," he said. "Are you hungry?"

"Starved," she admitted as she sat up in bed.

Then she realized she was still nude, and she yanked at the sheet, a hot flush surging up her neck and to her cheeks.

Piers caught her hand, stopping the sheet from its upward climb. "Don't be shy with me. I've seen and tasted every inch of your sweet body."

She slowly uncurled her fingers and relaxed her tense shoulders. He leaned in and kissed her long and slow, his lips exploring hers. This fantasy he spun allured her, drew her in and surrounded her in its firm grip.

A night of making love, breakfast in bed, tender kisses and gentle words.

If only it were all real.

Was he playing with her? Toying with her emotions? How could he act with such caring when he thought she was a liar and a manipulator?

"I'd give a lot of pennies for your thoughts right now."

She blinked and looked up to see him staring intently at her. No, he didn't really want to know what she was thinking. It would put the frown he so often wore right back on his face, and right now, she enjoyed the odd tenderness in the dark depths of his gaze.

"I'm thinking this is a nice way to wake up," she said with a smile.

He rubbed his thumb over her bottom lip and then trailed his fingers over her cheek, pushing back the wayward strands of her hair.

"Eat your breakfast. Your appointment is in two hours."

An appointment she'd forgotten in the aftermath of her wedding. She was scheduled for a sonogram as part of her pre-op workup. Afterward, she'd have more blood drawn and talk to the scheduling clerk about when she would be admitted to the hospital.

He placed the tray over her legs then handed her the utensils. "I'm going to go shower and shave. I have a few calls to make, and then I'll drive you to your appointment."

She glanced at his lean jaw, shadowed by the night's growth. Unable to resist, she lifted fingers to touch the hard edge of his chin and brushed the tips over the rough surface. His eyes closed as he leaned into her palm.

"Thank you."

He pulled away. "You're welcome. I'll leave you to eat now."

She watched as he walked away, his long stride eating up the floor. Despite the fact she had a delicious meal in front of her, her thoughts were of Piers in the shower, water sluicing over his muscled body. If she were daring, she'd go join him, but she had to admit, she had reservations about approaching him. So far, she'd allowed him to make the moves. It gave her an opportunity to study him and to figure out more about this man who'd upended her life.

Again she looked down at the sparkling diamond on her third finger. The weight was odd. She hadn't grown used to it yet, but she was fascinated by the sight and also by the meaning. In many ways it was a stamp of possession. She belonged to someone.

Realizing she'd spent too much time daydreaming, she hurriedly ate. After showering and dressing, she ventured downstairs where she found Piers in his study on the phone.

When he looked up and saw her standing at the door, he held up one finger to signal he'd be just a minute and then turned back to the phone.

Not wanting to intrude, she retreated back to the living

room to wait. He wasn't long. He was tucking his phone into his pocket when he strode into the living room.

"I've arranged for a chef for the time we're here. He'll arrive this afternoon in time to prepare tonight's dinner."

"You didn't really need to do that. I was only teasing."

"On the contrary. It was an excellent idea. You certainly don't need to be on your feet cooking, and if it was left to me, I'm afraid you'd grow tired of my limited culinary repertoire."

"You're shamelessly spoiling me," she protested, though it sounded weak even to her.

He half-smiled, something flickering in his eyes. It was that same look he always seemed to wear around her. "That's the idea." He looked down at his watch. "Are you ready? We ought to leave now in case traffic is bad."

She nodded and rose from her perch on the couch.

When they arrived for her appointment, Piers surprised her by staying at her side every step of the way. She'd imagined that he might sit in the waiting room, but he went back and listened with concentration to everything the nurse and the doctor had to say.

When it came time for her sonogram, Piers was like a child in a candy store. He studied each image, and one time he almost touched the screen.

"Is that her?" he asked as he pointed to one tiny fist.

The sonogram tech smiled. "She's sucking her thumb. Here's her chin," he said, tracing a small curve on the screen. "Here's her fist. She's got her thumb in her mouth."

Tears simmered in Jewel's eyes as she stared in awe at her child. "She's beautiful."

Piers turned to her, his voice husky and oddly emotional. "Yes, she is *yineka mou*. Very beautiful like her mother."

"What about the cyst?" Jewel asked anxiously. "Has it gotten smaller?"

"Unfortunately no. I'll have to compare the measurements to the last we recorded, but I think it's grown a little larger."

Jewel's face fell, and she closed her eyes. Somehow she'd hoped for a small miracle. That maybe the cyst would shrink so she wouldn't have to undergo surgery. She didn't want to risk anything that would harm her baby.

Piers found her hand and squeezed reassuringly. "We'll speak with the doctor and all will be well."

She clung to him, basking in his confidence. She needed it desperately because hers was flagging.

The sonogram tech rolled the portable machine out of her room, and she and Piers waited in anxious silence. He seemed far too calm, but then what did she expect? He didn't want this child. Didn't even believe it was his.

But he's here.

That meant something, didn't it?

The silence was disturbed when the doctor came back in, his expression pensive as he studied her chart.

"Miss Henley, it's good to see you again."

Piers cleared his throat. "It's Mrs. Anetakis now. I'm her husband, Piers." He thrust out his hand to shake the doctor's, and Jewel blinked as she watched Piers take control of the situation.

He and the doctor spoke of her condition and upcoming surgery as if she weren't in the room. At first she listened in befuddlement, and then anger stirred. This was her health, her child.

"I will decide when the surgery is to be scheduled," she said fiercely.

Piers touched her once on the knee. "Of course, *yineka*

mou. I am merely trying to understand all that is at stake here."

She flushed, sure she sounded petty and difficult, but she could literally feel the threads of her life slipping away, becoming permanently tangled in his.

"It should be done soon, Mrs. Anetakis," the doctor said. "I've consulted with a colleague of mine who will be assisting. It's a delicate surgery to be sure, but we feel confident of its success."

"And my baby?" she whispered.

He offered a soothing smile. "Your child will be fine."

"All right."

As they prepared to leave, the nurse gave Jewel instructions for when to report to the hospital. The entire thing scared her to death. Before she'd been able to put it out of her mind, but now it was there, staring her in the face.

"Come," Piers said quietly. He guided her toward his car and settled her inside.

For the first several miles, they drove in complete silence. Jewel stared out at the passing scenery, her mind occupied with the coming surgery.

"Tell me something. If you could live anywhere, anywhere at all, where would it be?"

Startled by the unexpected question, she turned to look at him. "The beach, I suppose." She smiled suddenly. "I've always dreamed of one of those big houses that overlooks the beach from a cliff." Her eyes closed as she imagined the sound of the waves crashing on the rocks. "A patio to watch the sun set in the evenings. What about you?"

His eyes never left the road, but she could feel him tense slightly.

"I've never given it much thought."

"Where did you live before? I mean before all this?"

A sardonic smile quirked his lip. "I don't have a permanent residence. I travel often and when I'm not away on business, I choose one of my hotels and I stay there."

"Your life sounds a lot like mine."

He cocked his head to the side and glanced at her for a moment. "How so?"

She shrugged. "No home."

He frowned as though he'd never had such a thought. And then his lips twisted ruefully. "I suppose you're right. Indeed I have many residences but no home. Perhaps you can solve that for me, *yineka mou*."

They pulled into the long drive to the house, but it wasn't until they came to a stop in the circle drive that Jewel saw the car parked in front of them. Was Piers expecting more company?

Then her gaze traveled to the front entrance and to the man sitting on the steps by the door.

"Kirk!"

As soon as the car stopped, she flew out and ran toward her friend.

Kirk rose when he saw her, a deep scowl on his face. But he caught her as she ran into his arms and hugged her fiercely.

"What the devil is going on, Jewel?" he demanded.

"I think that should be what I'm asking," Piers said coolly.

Jewel turned to see Piers staring at them, his eyes steely.

"Piers, this is a good friend of mine, Kirk. Kirk, this is Piers…my husband."

Kirk swore. "Damn it, Jewel, I told you to wait until I got here."

She swung back around to Kirk. "What are you talking about?"

"I e-mailed you after you e-mailed me telling me your

situation and that you were marrying this guy." He made an angry sweeping motion toward Piers.

"But I didn't get any e-mail. I swear. I had no idea if you'd even get mine."

Piers stepped to Jewel's side and wrapped an arm around her. He held her so tightly that she couldn't move.

"And did you rush all this way to offer us your congratulations?" Piers asked smoothly. "I'm sorry to say you missed the ceremony."

Kirk frowned even harder. "I'd like to talk to Jewel alone. I'm not leaving here until she convinces me that this is what she wants."

"Anything you have to say in front of my *wife,* can be said in front of me."

"Piers, stop," she said sharply. "Kirk is a very dear friend, and I owe him an explanation." She pried herself away from Piers and laid her hand on Kirk's arm. "Have you eaten anything?"

Kirk shook his head. "I hopped a flight and came straight here."

"Come in then. We can go out on the patio to eat, and we can talk."

She could have broken a stone on Piers's face. Without a word, he turned and stalked away, disappearing into the house.

"Nice guy," Kirk muttered.

Jewel sighed. "Come on in. I'll get us something to eat."

Eleven

Piers stood in the living room, sipping his drink and staring broodingly to the terrace where Jewel sat entertaining her guest.

Just who was this Kirk to her? Was he the father of her child? Had he left her high and dry and now had a change of heart? For all he knew, the two of them could be taking him on the ride of his life.

His eyes narrowed when he saw Jewel smile and then laugh at something Kirk had said. Then they both stood and Kirk drew her into his arms, hugging her tightly.

Piers's fingers curled into tight fists at his side. Then, before they returned inside, he walked away, determined not to give her the satisfaction of rising to her bait.

He was halfway across the room when he realized what he was doing. Running. That made him more furious than the thought of her making a fool of him. No woman was going to force him into retreat.

He turned to face them when the French doors opened. His gaze swept coldly over Kirk and then Jewel. She answered him with a frown, her eyes reproachful.

"Everything cleared up?" he asked mildly.

"Not really," Kirk said in a tight voice. "I've offered my assistance to Jewel so that her only alternative isn't marriage to you."

"How kind, only it's too late. She's my wife."

"Divorces are easy enough to get."

"I suppose they are, providing I was willing. I'm not."

"Stop it, both of you," Jewel demanded. "Kirk, please. I appreciate your help more than you know, but Piers is right. It's too late. We're married, and I want to make the best of it."

Kirk's expression softened as he looked at Jewel. "If you need anything at all, get in touch with me. It might take me a few days to get to you, but I'll be there, okay?"

Jewel smiled and hugged him tightly. "Thank you, Kirk. I appreciate everything you've done and for letting me stay in the apartment."

So it was Kirk's apartment and not Jewel's. She obviously hadn't been exaggerating when she said she had no money and no place to stay.

Guilt crowded into his mind again at the idea of her alone and in desperate need of help.

Kirk kissed her forehead and then pulled away. "If you're sure there isn't anything I can do, I'm going to head back to the airport and see if I can hop a flight today. If I'm lucky, I can be back on location in a day and a half."

"I'm just sorry you made the trip for nothing. If I'd gotten your e-mail, I would have told you not to bother coming."

Piers fought to maintain a neutral expression. Deleting the e-mail had backfired on him. If she was telling the truth.

She walked Kirk to the door, and they both disappeared outside. A few minutes later, Piers heard the car drive away and then Jewel came back inside, her expression stormy.

"What the hell was all that about?" she demanded.

He raised an eyebrow at the force of her anger. She was bristling from head to toe and her eyes shot ocean-colored daggers at him.

"Funny, I should be asking you that question."

"What are you talking about? Kirk is a good friend of mine. The only friend I have. If you have a problem with that, you can take a hike."

"So fiercely loyal," he murmured. "I wonder, though, if that loyalty extends to me?"

"Cut the crap, Piers. If you want a fight, let's fight, but I don't have time for little psychological games."

"Is that what we're doing? Fighting? It's a little soon for our first marital spat, wouldn't you say?"

"Go to hell."

With that, she turned and stomped up the stairs. A few seconds later, the door to her bedroom slammed with enough force to shake the house.

So she had a temper. He'd purposely baited her for no other reason than his anger over his apparent jealousy. The woman had him tied in knots, and he didn't like that one little bit.

If this Kirk was so hot to trot to come to Jewel's aid, where had he been when she really needed him? If he was the father of her child, had he deserted them both and was now only back because he had competition? Or was this an elaborate hoax for them both to con him out of a fortune? He must have played right into Jewel's hands when he offered her a generous settlement if the child turned out not to be his and they divorced. It was probably her plan all along.

But then the entire scheme hinged on him granting her a divorce. He smiled coldly. He couldn't wait to inform her that there would *be* no divorce.

Dinner was quiet and strained. Jewel was still furious over the way Piers had acted toward Kirk, and Piers's face was cast in stone. He ate as though nothing had occurred between them at all, and that made her even angrier. How were they supposed to have an argument when he didn't cooperate?

Dessert was served, and as much as she wanted to enjoy the decadent chocolate tart, it tasted like sawdust.

"I've been thinking," Piers said. He spoke coldly, with no warmth or inflection in his voice.

She didn't answer and continued to concentrate on dissecting her dessert.

"I no longer feel that divorce is an option."

Shocked, she dropped her fork, and winced at the loud clatter. "What? You believe that the baby is yours now? Before we get the results?"

He raised an eyebrow in a manner meant to make her feel inferior and at a disadvantage. It was mocking, almost as if he were laughing at her.

"I'm not a fool, Jewel. You'd do well to remember that."

"Then why this nonsense about a divorce? The child is yours, but you've never been inclined to believe that. Why on earth would you suggest there be no divorce until you're sure?"

"Maybe I'm just letting you know that your plan won't work. I won't grant a divorce, regardless of whether the child is mine."

He seemed to be studying her, waiting for a reaction. What kind of reaction? What was he thinking now?

And then it hit her like a ton of bricks. Her mouth fell open in disgust.

"You think this is a scheme to extort money from you. You think that Kirk is the father, and that I'm some whore sleeping with both of you."

She hadn't imagined that anyone had the power to hurt her anymore. Long ago, she'd developed impenetrable armor against the kind of pain other humans inflicted. Despite it all, hurt overwhelmed her. She felt betrayed even though she never imagined she had his loyalty.

With shaking legs, she clumsily got out of her chair, shoving it backward with more force than was necessary. She was determined not to break down in front of him. Before she escaped the room, she turned one last time to him.

"Who did this to you, Piers? Who made you into a bastard who won't trust anyone, and how long will it take you to figure out that I'm not her?"

She hurried away, no longer able to stand his brooding gaze.

Instead of retreating upstairs, she let herself out the French doors and ventured into the gardens. A chill chased away the flush of anger, and she gathered her arms close to her as she walked down a spiraling pathway deeper into the heart of the greenery.

Old-fashioned street lamps lit most of the paths. Finally she found a round, stone table with a circular bench. It was the perfect place to sit and enjoy the night air.

What had she done? She rubbed her stomach absently, thinking about her daughter and the future. A future that didn't seem quite as bright as it had before. Piers was being vengeful over a perceived wrong she hadn't dealt him, and so he'd decided, as if she had no choice or say in the matter, that there wouldn't be a divorce.

Oh, she knew according to his stipulations that there would never be a divorce because she knew the child was his. Only he seemed convinced otherwise.

What kind of life had she consigned herself and her child to? Would Piers's attitude soften toward their daughter when he learned the truth? And what about Jewel? Would she forever be relegated to just being the woman who gave birth to his daughter or would he soften toward her as well?

"You shouldn't be out here alone."

She whirled around, her anger surging back when she saw Piers standing there, hands shoved insolently into his pockets.

"I'm hardly alone, am I? No doubt there are countless security men surrounding me."

He nodded as he walked closer. "Yes, but you shouldn't take such a risk just because I have a security detail."

"Tell me, Piers, will your security detail protect me from you?" she asked mockingly.

"Interesting choice of words. I feel as though I'm the one in need of protecting."

She turned away, her shoulders shaking. "I want out, Piers. Immediately."

She heard his swift intake of breath and his hiss of anger.

"I've just told you I won't grant you a divorce."

"At this point, I couldn't care less. It isn't as if I ever intend to marry again. I just want to be away from you. Keep your damn settlement. I don't want anything from you. Just my freedom. I'll leave immediately."

She lurched forward, taking the spiraling pathway that

would lead her back to the house, but Piers was beside her in an instant, his hand tight around her arm.

"You can't go anywhere at this hour, Jewel. Be sensible."

"Sensible?" She laughed. "Now you tell me to be sensible. I should have been sensible the moment you walked back into my life and took it over."

"Stay until morning. You won't have to concern yourself with me asserting my husbandly rights."

"And you'll let me go?" she asked incredulously.

"If you still want to, then yes."

She studied him in the dark, and shook her head at the emotionless set to his face. Did he feel anything ever? Did he have a soul or had he given it away long ago?

"All right then. I'll leave first thing in the morning. Now if you'll excuse me, I'd like to go to bed."

Piers watched her go, his chest tight with something that felt remarkably like panic. Of all the reactions he might have expected, this wasn't one of them. When confronted with her deception, he'd expected tears, recriminations, even pleas to help her anyway. He hadn't expected her to tell him to go to hell and leave. Where was the profit in that?

Now he was stuck with thinking of a way to persuade her to stay. Until he figured out this puzzle, he needed her where he could find her at all times. For the first time, a surge of excitement tingled his nape. Could it be that she was really pregnant with his child? That this time, he had rights where the child was concerned?

If so, there was no way he would let Jewel walk out of his life.

Twelve

Unable to sleep, Jewel spent her time packing her clothing. She hadn't even unpacked everything yet, so the task didn't take her long. The rest of her time was spent sitting on the bed, her hands braced on the mattress as she silently stewed.

Why had she married Piers? It was a stupid decision, and yes, she'd been desperate, but not so desperate that she had called Kirk. No, she'd called *Piers* and then allowed him to take over and demand she marry him.

Face it. You're a hopeless dreamer.

All of the things she supposedly no longer believed in had guided her every step for the last five months. Was it any wonder she'd royally screwed up?

At two in the morning, she was lying in bed, in the dark, staring toward the window at the full moon spilling through the panes. She'd just closed her eyes and considered that she might finally fall asleep when sharp pain lanced through her side, stealing her breath with its intensity.

She drew her knees up in automatic defense, and another tearing pain ripped through her abdomen. She couldn't breathe, couldn't think, couldn't even process what she needed to do.

When the agony let up, she rolled toward the edge of the bed. Fear was as strong as the pain now. Fear for her child. Was she losing her baby?

Tears blurred her vision as she groped for a handhold. Her feet dangled above the floor when pain assaulted her again. She fell the rest of the way, landing with a thump on her side. She lay there, gasping for air, tears rolling down her cheeks as wave upon wave of pain shredded her insides.

Piers, she had to get to Piers.

She pushed her palm down on the surface of the floor, trying to lever herself up. The pain was unrelenting now. Nausea rolled through her stomach, swelling in her throat until she gagged.

She clamped her mouth shut and took deep breaths through her nose.

"Piers!"

It sounded weak, and her door was closed.

"Piers!" she said louder, and collapsed again when pain slashed through her side again.

Oh God, he wasn't coming. He probably couldn't hear her, and she couldn't get up.

Tears slipped faster down her cheeks, and she moaned helplessly as the tearing sensation overwhelmed her.

Then she heard the door fly open. The light flipped on, and footsteps thumped across the floor.

"Jewel! What's wrong? Is it the baby?"

Piers knelt beside her, his hands flying across her body and her stomach. He started to turn her, and she cried out in pain.

"Tell me what's wrong, *yineka mou*. Tell me how to help you," he said desperately.

"Hurt," she gasped out. "I hurt so much."

"Where?"

"My side, my stomach. Low—around my pelvis. God, I don't know. It hurts everywhere."

"Shhh, I'll take care of you," he said soothingly. "It'll be all right. I promise."

He gathered her in his arms and lifted her up.

"Will you be all right if I lay you on the bed for a moment? I need to get dressed, and then I'll drive you to the hospital."

She nodded against his chest, unable to form even a simple word.

He strode into his bedroom and settled her on the same bed they'd made love in the night before. His scent surrounded her, and oddly, offered her comfort.

It seemed to take him forever to dress, but finally he was back, pulling her to him. He hurried down the stairs and outside into the chilly night.

"I'm going to put you in the backseat so you can lie down," he murmured. "I'll have you at the hospital quickly. Try to hold on, *yineka mou*."

She curled into a ball as soon he put her down and clenched her fingers into tight fists to combat the urge to scream.

Not the baby. Please don't let it be the baby.

She barely registered the car stopping or Piers picking her up again. There were voices around her, a prick in her arm, the cold sheets of a bed, bright lights and then a strange man peering down into her eyes.

"Mrs. Anetakis, can you hear me?"

She nodded and tried to speak. Piers squeezed her hand—how long had he been there holding it?

"The cyst on your ovary has caused your tube to torque. I've called in your obstetrician. He wants us to prep you for surgery."

A low whimper erupted from her throat. Piers moved closer to her, smoothing his free hand through her hair in a comforting gesture.

"It will be all right, *yineka mou*. The doctor has assured me that you will receive the best care. Our baby will be just fine."

Our baby, she thought drowsily. Had he said our baby or was she imagining it? She couldn't quite get her thoughts together. The pain had diminished and she felt like she was floating on a light cloud.

"What did you do to me?" she asked.

She heard a light chuckle from the nurse at her head.

"Just something to make you more comfortable. We'll be wheeling you in to surgery in just a moment."

"Piers?"

"I'm here, *yineka mou*." Again his hand stroked her hair, and she turned into his palm, her eyes fighting to stay open.

"You said our baby. You believe she's yours?"

There was a hesitation, and she blinked harder to keep him in focus. There were worry lines crowding his forehead. Was he concerned for the baby?

"Yes, she is mine," he said huskily. "She's our daughter, and you'll take good care of her during the surgery, I'm sure. Rest now and don't try to speak. Let the medicine take the pain way."

She gripped his hand tightly, afraid that if she let go, he'd leave. The bed going into motion startled her, and she pulled his hand closer.

"Don't go."

"I'm not going anywhere," he said soothingly.

His lips brushed across her forehead, and she relaxed, closing her eyes and allowing the pain to leave her.

The voices dimmed around her. Then Piers kissed her again and told her softly that he would be waiting for her. Why? Where was he going? She wanted to ask but couldn't muster the energy to do anything more than lie there.

The bed rolled again and suddenly she was in a frigid room. She was lifted and transferred to a much harder surface, and it was cold. A cheerful voice sounded in her ear and asked her to count backward from ten.

She opened her mouth to comply but nothing came out. She even managed to open her eyes, but by the time she mentally made it to eight, everything went black.

Piers paced the confines of the surgery waiting room like a caged lion, edgy and impatient. He checked his watch again only to find that three minutes had passed since the last time he'd checked it. Damn it, how long would it take? Why weren't they telling him anything?

"Piers, how is she?"

Piers looked up to see Theron striding into the waiting room, his hair rumpled as if he'd rolled out of bed and onto the plane. But then he had. Piers felt guilty for dragging his brother out of bed in the middle of the night, but he was grateful to have him here.

Piers briefly embraced his brother and the two sat down.

"I don't know yet. They took her in a few hours ago, but I haven't heard anything since."

"What happened? Is the baby all right?"

"The cyst on her ovary caused a tubal torsion. She was in unspeakable pain so they took her to surgery to remove the cyst and probably the tube as well. She was scheduled for surgery in a week's time anyway so this just moved up the timeline."

"And the baby?"

"There are…risks, but they've assured me they'll do everything they can to prevent anything from happening to the baby."

"How long has she been in surgery?"

"Four hours," Piers said bleakly. "What could be taking so long?"

"You'll hear something soon," Theron said comfortingly. "Have you called Chrysander?"

Piers shook his head. "There was no need. It would take him too long to get off the island and come here. By the time he did, it would all be over with."

"Still, you should call him. He'd want to know, he and Marley both."

"I'll call them when I know how she is."

The two brothers sat in the waiting room. After a while Theron left and returned with coffee for the both of them. Piers sipped the lukewarm brew, not really tasting it.

"You're different, you know."

Piers looked up in surprise. "What are you talking about?"

"You seem more settled…more content even. I noticed it in your eyes when we were here for the wedding."

"As opposed to what?" he asked mockingly.

"As opposed to the way you've existed ever since Joanna screwed you over and left with Eric."

Piers flinched. No one ever mentioned Eric to his face. He was sure his family probably said a lot behind his back, but never when he was around. The pain was still too fresh.

"Don't ruin your chance at happiness, Piers. This is your chance to have it all."

"Or lose it all again. Maybe I already have."

"What do you mean?"

Piers took another gulp of the coffee and put the cup aside.

"She was going to leave me in the morning. Her bags were already packed when I found her on the floor in terrible pain."

"Want to talk about it?" Theron asked carefully. "I've been accused of being dense once or twice by a certain woman in my life."

"You seem so sure it's me who is the problem," Piers said dryly.

"You're a man, and men are always in the wrong. Haven't you learned anything yet?"

The corner of Piers's mouth lifted in a smile. Then he sobered. "I was an ass."

"Yes, well, it won't be the last time. It seems an inherent part of our genetic makeup."

"A male friend of hers showed up yesterday to come to her rescue. I didn't take it very well."

"No one can blame you for that. It's part of being territorial."

Piers snorted. "Next you'll be telling me that we're all cavemen stomping around and marking our territory like dogs."

"Quite an image you've conjured there, little brother. I imagine that's precisely what we do, just not in the literal sense."

Theron glanced sideways at Piers.

"So she was going to leave you because you didn't appreciate her male friend showing up?"

"I might have accused him of fathering her child and the two of them of running a scam to extort money from me."

Theron winced. "Damn, when you decide to pull off the gloves, you go for the full monty."

"As I said, I was an ass. I was angry. I told her that I wouldn't grant her a divorce, and she told me to take my settlement and go to hell."

"Doesn't sound much like a woman after your money does it?"

He'd thought the same thing himself.

"I want to trust her, Theron."

"And that frightens you."

And there it was in a nutshell. Funny how his brother cut so quickly to the heart of the matter. Yes, he wanted to trust her, but he was afraid, and it infuriated him.

"I don't want to ever allow a woman that much power over me again."

Theron sighed and put his hand on Piers's shoulder. "I understand, really I do. But you can't shut yourself away from the world for the rest of your life just because you got hurt once."

"Hurt?" Piers made a derisive sound. "I wish it was only hurt. She took from me what I loved most in the world. Somehow that goes beyond simple hurt."

"Still, as cliché as it sounds, life goes on. I want you to be happy, Piers. Chrysander and I worry about you. You can't go on traveling from one hotel to another your entire life. At some point you need to settle down and start a family. Jewel has given you that opportunity. Perhaps you should make the most of it. Give her a chance."

"Mr. Anetakis."

Both men yanked their heads up as a nurse appeared in the waiting room.

"Mrs. Anetakis is out of surgery. You can visit her in recovery for a moment if you like."

Piers shot up and hurried over to the nurse. "Is she all right? The baby?"

The nurse smiled. "Mother and baby are fine. The surgery went well. The doctor will stop in to talk to you in recovery before she's taken to a room. She's going to be very groggy, but you can talk to her for a moment if you like."

"I'll wait here," Theron said. "You go ahead."

"Thank you," Piers said sincerely. Then he turned to follow the nurse to see Jewel.

Thirteen

Her pain was different. It wasn't as agonizingly sharp as before. Instead it had settled to a dull ache, not as deep as it had been, but on the surface. Jewel tried to shift and gasped when it felt as though her belly had been ripped in two.

"Careful, *yineka mou*. You mustn't try to move. Tell me what it is you need, and I will help you."

Piers. She opened her eyes, squinting as the light speared her eyeballs. She quickly shut them again and cautiously opened them a slit as she tried to bring him into focus.

And then she remembered.

"The baby," she whispered. She reached her hands out in panic, feeling for her belly then gasping as more pain crashed through her system.

Piers took her hands and pulled them gently away from her belly.

"The baby is fine, as are you. See?" He carefully levered one of her hands to the swell of her belly but wouldn't allow her to exert any pressure.

She looked down at the unfamiliar feel of bulky bandages, but the swell was still evident. Tears flooded her eyes as her insides caved in relief.

"I was so afraid. I can't lose her, Piers. She's everything to me."

He cupped her cheek and rubbed his thumb over the damp trail underneath her eye. "Your surgery was a success. The doctor says the baby is doing well. They've been monitoring you for contractions." He gestured toward a machine at the side of her bed. "See? You can see and hear her heartbeat."

She turned her head and tuned into the soft *whop whop whop* sound that echoed in the still room.

"It's really her?"

Piers smiled. "Yes, our daughter is making her presence known."

She caught her breath as suddenly she remembered the scene just before they'd taken her to surgery. At first she thought surely she'd imagined it, but no, here again he was staking his claim. Why had he changed his mind?

"Thank you for getting me here so quickly," she said in a low voice. "I was so afraid I wouldn't be able to get to you."

He sobered as he gazed intently at her, his dark eyes seeming to absorb her. "You wouldn't have suffered for as long as you did if I had been there with you. From now on, you'll sleep in my room in my bed so if anything like this happens again, I'll know immediately. I don't like to think what could have happened if I hadn't heard you call out."

She processed his statement, blinking the cloudiness

from her mind. Everything was so fuzzy, and he confused her more than ever. It was as if their argument had never happened, as though he hadn't accused her of trying to pawn off another man's child on him.

"There will be plenty of time to talk later," he chided gently. "You're worn out and in pain. You need rest. I'll be here when you wake up. You can ask the questions I see burning in your eyes then."

She shook her head and winced when the movement caused a ripple of pain through her belly. "No, I have to know now. You said—implied—some terrible things, Piers. I won't stay with a man who thinks so little of me, not even for my daughter. Kirk is willing to help me get back on my feet. I should have called him in the first place."

"But you didn't," he said mildly. "You called me, as you should have. I think it best if we leave Kirk out of the equation."

She started to protest but he held a finger over her lips.

"Shhh, don't upset yourself. I owe you an apology, *yineka mou.* I'm sure it won't be the last I ever have to offer you. I would appreciate your patience with me. I'm not an easy man. I realize this. I should not have implied what I did. From this day forward, we go on as a family. You're having my child. We owe it to her to be a solid parental unit, not one where I continually upset you and cause you such stress. If you'll give me another chance, I'll prove to you that our marriage will work."

She stared at him in absolute stupefaction. His sincerity was etched on his face. His eyes burned with it. There was no arrogance to his voice, just simple regret.

Something inside her chest, perilously close to her heart, unfurled and loosened. Forgotten for a brief moment

was the pain that throbbed in her abdomen and the fuzzi-
ness caused by the pain medication. Warmth, blessed and
sweet, hummed through her veins. Hope. It had been so
long since she'd felt such a thing that she hadn't identified it at first. For the first time, she had hope.

He drew her hand to his mouth and pressed a soft kiss
inside her palm. "Do you forgive me? Will you give me
another chance to make things right?"

"Yes, of course," she whispered, her voice so shaky that
her words came out in barely a croak.

"And you'll stay? There'll be no more talk of leaving?"

She shook her head, too choked to say anything more.

"You won't regret it, *yineka mou,*" he said gravely. "We
can make this work. We can do this."

She smiled and then grimaced as pain radiated from the
center of her body. Piers leaned forward, directing her attention to the small device lying beside her on the bed. He
picked it up and pressed it into her palm.

"This is for pain. You press the button here, and it injects
a small amount of medication into your IV. You can press
it every ten minutes if you have the need."

He depressed the button himself, and a split second
later, she felt the slight burn as it entered her vein. The
relief was almost instantaneous.

"Thank you."

"I will take care of you and our baby," he said solemnly.
"I don't want you to worry about a thing except to get
better."

She smiled up at him, her eyelids fluttering sleepily.

"Tired," she said in a half murmur.

"Then sleep. I'll be right here."

She turned toward his voice, and when he started to move
his hand from hers, she curled her fingers around his,

keeping them laced. He relaxed and tightened his grip on her hand.

"When am I getting outta here?" she mumbled as she fought the veil of sleep.

He chuckled lightly. "There's no hurry. You'll leave when the doctor feels it's safe for you to do so. In the meantime enjoy everyone fussing over you."

"Just you," she muttered just before she surrendered to the dark.

"Are you sure everything is prepared?" Piers said into his mobile phone as he entered Jewel's room.

Jewel looked up and smiled and Piers held up one finger to signal he would be finished shortly.

"Good. Very good. I owe you one, and I have no doubt that you'll collect."

He snapped his phone shut and hastened to Jewel's side. He bent down and brushed his lips across hers in greeting.

"How are my girls today?"

"Your daughter is very active, which is a blessing and a curse."

Piers gave her a sympathetic look. "Do her movements aggravate your incision?"

She grimaced. "I think she's playing target practice. She's has uncanny accuracy for kicking that precise spot."

"I'm sorry. I know it must be painful for you."

"The alternative doesn't bear thinking about, so I'm grateful for her movements."

"Has the doctor been by to see you yet?"

"He came by while you were out. He said if all goes well today and I have no further contractions, that I can be released tomorrow. I'm to be on strict bed rest for a week

and then I can get up and around as long as I don't
overdo it."

"And I will see to it that you obey his instructions to
the letter."

She was careful not to laugh, but she grinned in amusement. "Why do I get the feeling you're going to enjoy my
convalescence?"

He gave her an innocent look. "Why would you think
such a thing?"

"Because you're a man used to bossing people around
and having them obey you implicitly," she said darkly.

"You say this as if it was a bad thing."

This time she did chuckle and promptly groaned when
her belly protested. Piers gave her a disapproving frown,
and she rolled her eyes.

The past several days had been good considering she
was stuck in a hospital bed. After the first day, the nurse
had come in to help her get up, and Jewel had spent fifteen
minutes trying to argue that there was no need for her to
get up when every movement nearly split her in two. It was
the threat of a catheter that finally gave her the motivation
to endure sitting up and standing.

Piers had been wonderful. The brooding man who'd so
insolently told her there would be no divorce had seemingly disappeared, and was replaced by someone who saw
to her every need. She had to admit that he was trying very
hard to put their past disagreements behind them.

A light knock sounded at the door, and to her surprise,
Piers's brothers and their wives crowded into her room.
She must have looked as mortified as she felt because
Piers squeezed her hand.

"Don't worry, *yineka mou*. You look beautiful. They
won't stay long enough to tire you. I'll see to it."

He was lying through his teeth, but she loved him for it.

The thought hit her between the eyes and was more painful than the stapled incision in her belly. Love? Dear God, she'd fallen in love with him.

She tried to smile, but what she wanted to do was crawl into a deep, dark hole. How could she have allowed herself to fall in love with him—with any man? Apparently she hadn't had enough hurt in her life. No, she obviously wanted to pile on more pain and disappointment.

It was all well and fine to want to be loved, but to offer her love on a silver platter? She was just asking for rejection.

"Jewel? Have we come at a bad time?" Marley asked quietly.

Jewel blinked and saw that the two couples were standing at the foot of her bed, studying her intently.

"No. No, of course not. I'm sorry. I'm still a bit muddled. It's probably all the pain medication they've funneled through me."

Beside her Piers frowned, and she just hoped he'd remain quiet about the fact she hadn't had pain medication in three days. The doctor hadn't wanted her to be on any narcotic for an extended period of time. It was too risky for the baby.

She smiled brightly at Bella and Marley and opted to keep her gaze away from Chrysander and Theron. They intimidated the hell out of her, and she wasn't in the habit of giving up that kind of advantage to anyone.

"How are you feeling?" Bella asked as she moved forward.

She perched on the side of Jewel's bed and flipped her long dark hair over her shoulder.

"Has Piers been bullying you? Marley and I can take him outside and rough him up for you."

Jewel smiled and swallowed to keep from laughing.

"Don't make her laugh," Piers growled. "It hurts her too much. Besides, I have you and Marley wrapped around my finger, remember?"

Chrysander let out a loud guffaw. "Don't let him fool you, Jewel. All either woman has to do is look at this idiot brother of mine, and he gives them whatever they want, much to mine and Theron's dismay."

"As if you both don't spoil them shamelessly," Piers said dryly.

"That may be true, but a woman can never have too many men at her disposal," Marley said cheekily.

"There is only one man at your disposal, *agape mou*," Chrysander growled. "And you would do well to remember that."

Jewel watched the interaction between the three brothers and Bella and Marley, and for the first time, she didn't feel like an outsider. The horrible feeling of intense longing didn't hit her like it did the first time she'd met them. This time she felt more of an equal, as if she belonged in this intimate circle of family members.

"You must be feeling better," Bella said from her perch on the bed. "You're smiling so beautifully. You look quite radiant for someone who has just undergone surgery."

"It's the pregnancy," Theron said slyly. "A woman never looks more beautiful than when she is pregnant."

"Nice try," Bella said dryly. "Your flattery will get you nowhere. And if you start lusting after pregnant women, I'll make it so you'll never be able to father children."

Jewel couldn't help but laugh when Theron all but paled. She put her hand over her belly and groaned, but even amidst the pain, it felt so good to laugh. She felt lighter than she had in a long time.

"Are you all right?" Piers asked quietly.

She waved him off. "I'm fine. Truly." Then she turned to Bella. "Why do I get the feeling this is an ongoing battle between you and Theron?"

Bella grinned. "If Theron had his way, I'd have already popped out a veritable brood of children, but I'm too young, and we have so much to do together before I think of having babies. I'll eventually give in and fill his nursery, but until then I live to torment him."

Jewel studied Theron's face as Bella spoke. His eyes shone with love for his wife, and she knew that he didn't exert any real pressure. It was obviously a long-standing joke between them.

"Besides, Marley has taken it upon herself to provide enough Anetakis children for both of us," Bella added with a smirk.

Piers eyebrows shot up. "Marley?"

Marley blushed while Chrysander smiled smugly and wrapped his arm around her waist. It was a possessive gesture not lost on Jewel.

"You're pregnant again?" Piers demanded.

"In seven months she'll give me the daughter I want," Chrysander said arrogantly.

"And if it's another son?" Marley challenged.

Chrysander looked down at her, passion blazing in his eyes. "Then we'll simply try again until we get it right."

Marley and Bella both laughed, and Jewel joined them, holding her belly all the while.

What a marvelous family. A family that she was now a part of. It was simply too much to take in.

"We should probably go now," Chrysander said as he

studied Jewel. "You look as though you're in pain, and we don't want to tire you out. We simply wanted to come by to check in on you and to let you know that if there is anything you need, anything at all, just let us know. You're family now."

She stared back at him, tears in her eyes. "Please, don't go. You're not bothering me a bit. I've so enjoyed having you all."

"Tell me," Bella said, leaning forward to capture Jewel's attention. "Are they letting you have real food yet? I'm simply dying for some pizza. Theron thinks it's barbaric, and so I'm shamelessly using you as an excuse to get some really greasy, cheesy pizza."

"You call that real food?" Theron asked in mock horror.

"Oh I'd love pizza," Jewel said with real longing. "Double pepperoni and extra cheese. Oh, and light sauce if no one objects."

"Tell you what," Bella said. "We'll order one our way and let the rest fend for themselves. What you suggested sounds positively divine."

Jewel looked hopefully at Piers who sighed in resignation.

"What man can possibly say no to a woman when she looks at him that way?"

Both Theron and Chrysander laughed.

Chrysander clapped Piers on the back. "Now you're learning, little brother. Now you're learning."

Fourteen

"I have a surprise in mind," Piers said as he wheeled her out of the hospital's front entrance. "It will take a while to execute, so what I want you to do is relax and try to rest as much as possible."

A flutter of excitement bubbled in her stomach. She felt like a kid at Christmas. For someone who'd never gotten accustomed to any sort of surprise, she was fast finding she liked them very much. Or at least the anticipation of having one.

Piers's security detail stood outside the limousine awaiting their arrival. One opened the back door, and Piers scooped Jewel up from the wheelchair and carefully placed her in the seat, taking extra care not to jostle her. Then he walked around to the other side while all but one of his security team slipped into a car parked behind the limousine. The last man got into the front with the driver.

"Where are we going?" she asked curiously when they went the opposite direction of the house she and Piers had been staying in.

"The airport."

She raised her eyebrows. "Where are we going?"

Familiar excitement lit her veins. She loved to travel for the excitement of going to a new place, meeting new people and experiencing different cultures. Only this time she wasn't going alone, and that thrilled her more than she would have thought possible.

He smiled and reached over to take her hand. "If I told you, it would spoil the surprise."

"But my clothes, my things. I haven't packed."

"All taken care of," he said smoothly. "This is why I hire a staff."

"Did you pack my chef?" she asked mournfully. "He made the most delicious food."

Piers chuckled. "I assure you, you won't go hungry."

A while later they pulled up next to a small jet parked on a private airstrip. Piers waited while his security got out and boarded the plane. Then he walked around to her side and picked her up.

"I'll take her if you like, Mr. Anetakis," Yves offered. He was the only one who Jewel knew by name. The rest were a mystery to her, but then Yves seemed more of a personal bodyguard for Piers while the rest operated on the perimeter.

Piers shook his head. "Thank you Yves, but I'll take Mrs. Anetakis to the plane."

Each step he took was in careful consideration of her comfort. When he reached the steps to the plane, he ducked down and walked inside.

Never before had she seen the inside of a private jet, and

if she'd been expecting a smaller version of a regular airliner, she was mistaken. There were seats in the front covered in soft, supple leather that looked incredibly luxurious and comfortable. Beyond them was a sitting area with a recliner and a couch along with a coffee table, television and a mini bar.

Piers followed the direction of her gaze. "After we take off, I'll show you the rest. There's a bedroom in the back of the plane that you can lie down in. There's also a small kitchenette, so if you want anything, you've only to let the flight attendant know."

Her eyes widened. "Flight attendant? You have one for the plane?"

"Of course. She travels with the pilot. They're a husband and wife team. It's an arrangement that suits them well. Now, would you like a window or an aisle seat?"

"Window," she said.

He carefully settled her in place and then took the seat next to her. Before fastening his seat belt, he reached over and gingerly buckled hers into place, leaving it loose around her belly.

The flight attendant walked up with a smile and greeted Piers. Then she turned her smile on Jewel. "I'm very happy to meet you, Mrs. Anetakis. If there is anything I can get you during the flight, don't hesitate to ask. We'll be cleared for take off shortly. Would you like something to drink while you wait?"

Jewel shook her head. "No thank you. I'm fine for now."

Minutes later, they taxied down the runway and took off. Jewel leaned her head on Piers's shoulder and snuggled into his warmth. As curious as she was to see the rest of the plane, getting up and moving hurt too much.

She was perfectly content to remain here for the duration of the flight.

"You're still not going to tell me where we are?" Jewel asked several hours later as their car wound its way along a curving highway.

Piers smiled. "Patience, *yineka mou*. I think you'll find it's well worth the wait."

She sighed and relaxed in her seat. Wherever they were, it was beautiful and unspoiled. She'd lay odds it was in the Caribbean or some similar tropical place. Were they going to one of his hotels?

They stopped at a security gate where Piers punched in a code. Huge iron gates swung slowly open, and they continued up the drive.

Lush greenery abounded. It was like driving into a private paradise. Flowers, plants, fountains and even a mini waterfall cascaded over rocks in the distance.

And then she saw the house. Her mouth fell open at the sight of the stunning cottage, well if you could call something so huge a cottage. But despite its size, it had the look of a cozy, stone cottage. It looked positively homey.

"Is this where we're staying for the time being?" she asked when the car pulled to a stop beside another large fountain with flowers floating serenely in the pool surrounding it.

"This is your house, *yineka mou*. It now belongs to us."

She was struck positively speechless.

"But the best is yet to come," he said.

She watched him walk around the front of the car and wondered how on earth it could get any better?

He helped her from the car and motioned his security men who were standing several feet away. They quickly disappeared while Piers put a strong arm around her waist and urged her toward a walkway leading around the house.

And then she heard it. The distant sounds of waves crashing. She inhaled deeply, catching the salty air in her nostrils.

"Oh Piers," she breathed.

They topped a small rise between a section of gardens and the wooden deck jutting from the house over a sharp cliff. She looked out and all she could see was a great expanse of ocean. Brilliant blue, so stunning it almost hurt her eyes to look at. It sparkled like a million sapphires.

The walkway continued, smooth in places and at other areas it became a series of steps leading down to the beach. The house was situated on the cliff in a secluded cove between two outcroppings. It afforded them a small stretch of sandy beach, completely private.

It was the most magnificent view she could have imagined. And it was theirs.

"I don't know what to say," she whispered. "This is my dream, Piers. I can't believe this is ours."

"It's yours, *yineka mou*. My wedding gift to you. I have it on good authority it comes equipped with a full staff, including a certain chef you've grown extraordinarily fond of."

She threw her arms around him, ignoring the painful jolt to her incision. "Thank you. It's so wonderful, Piers. I don't know how I'll ever be able to thank you."

"By taking good care of yourself and my daughter," he said seriously. "I don't want you taking the pathway down to the beach unless I'm with you."

"I promise," she said joyfully. Right now she'd promise him the moon.

"Come inside. Dinner has been held for us. We'll eat on the terrace and watch the sun go down."

She went eagerly, anxious to see the inside of the house. He gave her a quick tour of the downstairs before they walked onto the deck in the back. Their places had been set, and she eased into her chair to wait for the food.

"It's so gorgeous," she said in awe. She was completely and utterly overwhelmed by the knowledge that she lived here now, that this place was hers. It was all simply too good to be true.

"I'm glad you like it. I was afraid I wouldn't have everything in place before you were released from the hospital."

"You didn't already own it?"

"I had my representatives looking for just the perfect place the day you told me where you'd like to live more than anywhere else. When they found this place, I knew it was perfect. The sale isn't quite final, but I convinced the owner to allow us to take possession of it until all the paperwork can be finished."

She was unable to keep the wide smile from forming on her face. "That's the most wonderful thing anyone has ever done for me."

He put his hand over hers, his palm warm and soothing. "Tell me, *yineka mou*. Has anyone ever done a wonderful thing for you? I get the impression yours has not been an easy life."

She stiffened and tried to withdraw her hand, but he wouldn't allow it. His grip tightened around her fingers, but his touch stayed soothing the entire time.

"What is it you won't tell me?" he asked quietly. "Surely there should be no secrets between a man and his wife."

She turned away to stare at the ocean, the breeze blowing across her cheeks and drying the invisible tears she shed.

"It's nothing so dramatic," she said matter of factly. "My parents died when I was very young. I barely remember them, and even now I wonder if the people I remember aren't just one of the many foster families I was shuttled through."

"You had no relatives to take care of you?"

She shook her head. "None that would, anyway."

A young woman came out then carrying a tray of food, and Jewel sighed in relief. She didn't miss Piers's frown, which told her the conversation wasn't closed, just delayed.

Still, nothing good would come of her rehashing the past.

They ate in companionable silence. Jewel enjoyed the sounds and smells of the ocean and found herself more relaxed than she'd been in longer than she could remember.

As the sun dipped lower on the horizon, the sky faded to soft hues of pink and purple with threads of gold spreading from the disappearing sun. The ocean shimmered in the distance, reflecting the brilliance of the sunset.

She hadn't realized she'd long since stopped eating, so entranced by the view was she. Only when the maid returned to collect the dinner plates, did Jewel break from her reverie.

"You look tired, *yineka mou*," Piers said gently. "I think I should take you upstairs so you can get ready for bed."

She yawned and then chuckled at how easily she'd given herself away. "Bed sounds really good right now. Does the bedroom have windows we can open? I'd love to be able to hear the ocean."

"I think you'll find the view from our bedroom magnificent, and we can certainly open the windows if that is your wish."

He helped her to her feet and they returned inside. They took the stairs slowly, and she bit her lip when the upward movement put awkward pressure around the area of her incision. Her entire belly felt bruised and tender.

When they entered the master bedroom, she let out a sound of pure delight. The entire back wall that faced the ocean was glassed in from floor to ceiling. She left Piers's side to peer over the water, her palms pressed to the cool glass.

Her throat suspiciously tight, she turned to face Piers. "This has been the most wonderful day. Thank you so much."

"I'm glad you approve," he said huskily.

She returned her attention to the view, watching as the last bits of the orange glow from the sun disappeared into the sea.

"What about your work? Your hotels?"

He came to stand beside her, studying the ocean with her.

"Most of my work can be handled from here. I have a phone, my computer and a fax machine. There will be times I need to travel. Up to now, I've always done the bulk of the traveling, but I find myself unwilling to continue on that track. Either my brothers will have to help shoulder the load or we'll hire someone to do most of the traveling."

"You won't miss it?" she asked lightly.

"A few months ago I would have said yes, very much, but now I find myself more reluctant to be away from my wife and our child."

Warmth spread through her chest. How like a family

they sounded. She wasn't entirely certain what had caused him to change his tune, but she had no desire to question it. She only hoped it lasted.

Fifteen

For the next several days, Jewel rested and recovered under the watchful eye of Piers and the staff he'd hired. It seemed odd at first to have other people in the house, but they blended so seamlessly into the background that Jewel quickly became accustomed to their presence.

Piers even had a physician come to the house to check her incision and remove the staples so she wouldn't have to make the trip into town.

In short, she was spoiled and pampered endlessly, and she was fast becoming bored out of her mind. She was positively dying to explore her surroundings. A trip down to the beach was foremost on her wish list, but she also wanted to go beyond the grounds of their estate and see the rest of the island.

According to Piers, the island was small and not yet discovered by the many tourists that flocked to the Caribbean.

Fishing was the main source of industry for the locals. There were plans to build an elaborate resort, an exclusive playground for the wealthy where no expense would be spared and guests would be lavished with personal attention.

The goal was to keep the island as private and as unspoiled as possible while still providing an influx of capital for the locals.

Jewel broached the subject of a trip down to the beach over breakfast, the day after the doctor had removed her staples and pronounced her fit.

Piers frowned for a moment. "I'm not sure you should be descending the stairs this soon after your surgery, *yineka mou.*"

"But I'll have you to hang on to," she cajoled. "Please, Piers. I'm about to go stir-crazy. I've watched from a distance for so long, I'm beginning to feel like I'm viewing postcards."

He smiled. "I find I can deny you nothing. All right. After breakfast we'll go down to the beach. I'll have the cook prepare a picnic lunch."

She bounced on her seat like an excited child. "Thank you. I can't wait to see it!"

"Be sure and wear some comfortable shoes. I don't want you slipping on the steps."

She smiled at his solicitousness. How perfect things were right now. Gone was the feeling that at any moment her world could come crashing down around her. If only…if only he'd open up to her.

For days she'd argued with herself, vacillated from having the courage to ask and having it disappear. The other problem was that if she managed to get him to talk to her about his past then she'd be forced to speak of her own.

Soon, she promised herself. But not this morning. Nothing was going to ruin their outing to the beach.

Picnic basket in one hand, his other firmly wrapped around hers, Piers made his way down the steps carved into the face of the cliff. With each downward movement, the sounds of the ocean got louder and Jewel became more excited.

When their feet finally hit the sand, Jewel stopped and looked up at the impressive rocky cliffs looming over and around them, isolating their stretch of beach from the rest of the world.

"It's like we're in our own little world," she said in awe.

Piers smiled. "No one can see you except by boat, and I have it on good authority the locals don't fish this end of the island."

"Conjures up all sorts of naughty possibilities, doesn't it?"

His eyes glittered in response. "You can be sure once you are well that I'll be all too willing to indulge in some of those possibilities."

She laughed and kicked off her shoes, digging her toes into the warm sand. Unable to resist the lure of the foaming waves, she hurried toward the water's edge, anxious to feel the water swirling around her ankles.

The cascading water met her and rushed over her feet. She threw out her arms to embrace the breeze and smiled in absolute delight as her hair billowed behind her. Closing her eyes, she inhaled deep and wished she could stop time, right here in this perfect moment.

"You look like a sea nymph," Piers said. "More beautiful than a woman should be allowed to look."

She turned to see him standing beside her, his pants rolled up to his knees, his feet bare.

"Is it safe to swim here?"

He nodded.

"We'll have to do it sometime."

"You look happy, *yineka mou*. Have I made you so?"

The vulnerability that flashed in his dark eyes made her catch her breath. This strong, arrogant man was as human as the next person. Not questioning the wisdom of doing so, she flung herself into his arms, wrapping hers around his neck.

"You're so good to me, Piers. You do make me so very happy."

Tentatively, he returned her embrace and as she pulled her head away to look at him, their eyes met. Their lips were but an inch apart, and she licked hers nervously, in anticipation of what she knew was about to happen.

Instead of waiting on him, she pulled him close, fitting her mouth to his. He seemed willing to let her dictate the pace, and she explored his mouth thoroughly, learning every nuance, his taste, feeling the warmth of his tongue.

His fingers were a soft whisper against her neck. They delved farther into her hair, holding her closer as she deepened the kiss. The salt from the ocean danced on their tongues, mixing with the heady sweetness of their passion.

Finally she pulled away, gazing up at him through half-lidded eyes. "And do I make you happy?" she asked huskily.

He ran his thumb over her cheekbone, stroking to the corner of her mouth. "You make me very happy."

She smiled brilliantly at him then grabbed his hand and tugged him farther down the beach. "Come on! Let's explore."

Indulgently, he allowed to her to pull him along. They covered every inch of the beach from cliff to cliff. By the time they returned to where the picnic basket lay, she was starving.

"Help me with the blanket," she said as she unfurled the brightly colored quilt. Laughing, she fought with the billowing material as it refused to cooperate.

"Here, let me."

Piers wrestled the blanket to the sand and piled their shoes at each corner to hold it down.

"Now hurry and sit before it flies away again," he said.

She gingerly eased down and dragged the basket into the middle of the quilt. Piers sat beside her and they began divvying up the food.

The sun shone bright above them, and the sand glistened like tiny jewels, scattered to the water's edge. She sighed and turned her face up into the warmth.

"You look very content, *yineka mou*. Like a cat sunning herself."

"Haven't you ever wished that a single moment could last forever?"

He became pensive as though he were giving her question serious consideration. "No, I can't say I have, but if I were given to such flights of fancy, then today would be one such time."

She smiled. "It is perfect, isn't it?"

"Yes. It is."

They finished eating, and Jewel lay back on the blanket, enjoying the sounds and smells of the ocean. The warmth of the sun's rays lulled her to sleep, and before she knew it, she was being shaken awake.

"It's time to return to the house, *yineka mou*. The sun will be setting soon."

She yawned and blinked lazily as his face came into view. She smiled up at him and held up her hand so he could help her.

Together they collected the remnants of their lunch,

and Piers packed them and the blanket into the basket. He reached for her hand when they arrived at the bottom of the steps, and she slipped her fingers into his.

Tonight. Tonight she'd broach the subject of his past, and for the first time, she wouldn't avoid hers. She wanted to know his secrets, the source of the pain she saw lurking in the depths of those shuttered eyes.

Would he share those secrets or would he block her out? And should she press him on something that clearly he had no wish to discuss?

True to his word, after the night Piers had found Jewel on the floor of her bedroom writhing in pain, she'd slept each night in his bed. In deference to her incision, he spooned against her back, and she enjoyed the warmth and security his muscled body offered.

Most nights she wondered if they'd resume their love-making after the tenderness left her abdomen. Tonight, however, she lay there, cuddled against his chest, gathering her courage to broach the subject of his past.

"Piers?"

"Mmm-hmm."

Carefully she started to turn over to face him.

"Will you tell me who hurt you so badly?"

He went still, and she wished the lamp was on so she could gauge his reaction.

"Who made you so distrustful of women?" she continued on. "And why is it that you don't want this to be your child."

He put a finger on her lips. "That's where you're wrong, *yineka mou*. I want her to be mine very much."

Jewel cocked her head to the side. "But you seem so convinced that she isn't."

He turned on his back to stare up at the ceiling. She tentatively cuddled into the crook of his arm and laid her head on his shoulder. When he didn't resist, she relaxed, allowing her fingers to trail through the hairs on his chest.

"Ten years ago I met and fell in love with a woman. Joanna. I was young and stupid and convinced I had the world by the tail."

"Don't we all at that age," she said with a slight smile.

He chuckled. "I suppose you're right. Anyway, she became pregnant, and so we married right away."

Jewel winced at the similarities but remained quiet as he continued.

"She gave birth to a boy. We named him Eric. I adored him. I was as happy as a man can be. I had a beautiful wife who seemed devoted to me. I had a son. What more could I ask for?"

Jewel's mouth turned down unhappily. She could only imagine what he'd say next.

"And then one day I came home to find her packing. Eric was two years old. I remember him crying the entire time I tried to reason with Joanna. I couldn't understand why she was leaving. There hadn't seemed to be any problems. I had no warning.

"Finally, when I told her that she could leave but there was no way in hell I'd let my son go, she told me that he wasn't my child."

Jewel sucked in her breath. "And you believed her?"

A derisive sound escaped his lips. "No, I didn't believe her. But to make a long story short, her lover who she was involved with when she and I met had devised the perfect plan to milk me for all they could. Several months and a paternity test later, it was proved that Eric wasn't my son. Joanna took him and a great deal of my money, and I haven't seen either since."

"Oh Piers, I'm so sorry," she whispered. "How horrible of her to allow you to fall in love with a child you thought was yours and then to yank him so cruelly away. How could she do that to either of you?"

Piers trailed his fingers up and down her bare arm.

"I have nightmares sometimes. I hear Eric calling to me, asking why I won't help him, why I left *him*. All I can remember is the day they left, and how Eric screamed and cried, how he stretched his arms out trying to get to me, and all I could do was watch her walk away with my son. It's a sight I'll never get out of my mind."

"You miss him."

"He was my entire world for those two years," he said simply. "I realize now that I didn't love Joanna. I was infatuated with her, but I did love Eric."

Jewel rose up and cupped his cheek in her palm as she lowered her mouth to his. Then she drew his hand down to her swollen belly where their daughter bumped and turned between them.

"She's yours, Piers. Yours and mine."

"I know, *yineka mou*. I know."

Sixteen

"Piers looks more at ease than I've ever seen him," Marley said to Jewel as the two stood on the patio overlooking the ocean.

Jewel turned to the other woman and smiled. "Really? I hope I can take credit for it."

Bella laughed as she took another sip of her wine. "Of course the credit is yours. I'd swear the man is in love."

Jewel bit her lip and turned away. She wanted Piers to love her, but he'd never said the words. She wasn't sure he was capable of offering his love to another woman after what had happened with Joanna.

"Your house is beautiful, Jewel," Marley said. "I just wish it wasn't so far away from Greece."

"Or New York," Bella said dryly. "You think Piers planned it this way?"

Jewel grinned. "But we have jets at our disposal, don't we?"

"Hmm, you're right," Marley said thoughtfully. "The world shrinks quite a bit when airplanes are involved. No reason we couldn't all meet in New York for some shopping. Theron is a soft touch, and he'd no doubt accommodate us."

Bella glared over at Marley. "Just because he isn't an ape swinging from tree to tree and beating his chest while muttering stuff like 'you my woman' doesn't mean he's a softy."

"She's very protective and possessive when it comes to Theron," Marley said with a roll of her eyes. "All I meant was that of the three brothers, Theron would be the most accommodating when it comes to us wanting to get together. Chrysander and Piers would spend a month planning the security team."

Bella nodded. "You're right about that."

Jewel looked at the two women in question. "Piers mentioned what had happened to Marley when I asked him why the need for all the security people. Has nothing been resolved yet?"

Marley sighed unhappily. "As a matter of fact, we think the men who kidnapped me have been arrested. Chrysander got the call yesterday but we didn't want to ruin our time here. When we leave, we're flying back to New York with Bella and Theron so that I can identify the suspects."

Bella threaded her arm around Marley's waist and squeezed. "I'm so sorry, Marley. What rotten timing for you when you've been so ill with the new baby."

Marley smoothed a hand over her still flat stomach. "Chrysander is worried it will be too much, and he's still feeling so guilty. He hates that I have to do this."

Jewel touched her hand in a comforting gesture. "Still, what a relief to know that they've been apprehended. I can only imagine the fear you've been living in."

"And the inconvenience it's caused you and Bella," Marley added. "I know that Theron and Piers have taken extra precautions because of the potential threat to anyone close to them. Maybe we can all relax a little now."

Bella held up her glass in a toast. "To freedom and relaxation."

Jewel held up her glass of water as did Marley and the women clinked the crystal.

"I'm so glad you're all here," Jewel said.

Bella looped her arm through Jewel's. "We're grateful you've made Piers so happy. He's been so…hard."

Marley nodded. "It took him a long time to accept me. Of course now he'd do just about anything if I needed him, but it wasn't like that in the beginning."

Jewel sobered. "Marley, do you think you could pull Chrysander to the side for me? There is something I'd like to discuss with him, something I'd prefer Piers not to know right now."

Marley lifted a brow. "Okay, I can do that, but you should know that Bella and I are insatiably nosy, and you'll have to fill us in first."

Jewel laughed and squeezed Marley's hand with her free one. "I'll tell you after Chrysander. That way you two don't try to talk me out of it."

"Uh-oh," Bella said with a groan. "I don't like the sound of that."

"I'm too curious to try and dissuade her," Marley said. "If you'll stay out here Jewel, Bella and I will make sure Piers is occupied while you talk to Chrysander."

"Thank you."

The two women disappeared indoors leaving Jewel to gaze out over the sea. She was so absorbed by the view, that she didn't hear Chrysander when he came out.

"Marley tells me you'd like to speak with me."

Startled, she made a quick turn, and swallowed as she stared back at Piers's older brother. He raised a brow in surprise.

"Do I frighten you, Jewel?"

"Oh no, of course not…okay, yes, you do," she admitted.

"It is certainly not my intention," he said formally. "Now tell me, what can I do for you?"

She twisted her fingers nervously in front of her. This was probably a stupid idea, and Chrysander would probably tell her she was out of her mind. He might even be angry that she intended to pry into Piers's past.

"Piers told me about Joanna…and Eric."

Chrysander's eyes grew cold.

"I know how hurt he was by what happened."

Chrysander sighed and moved closer to Jewel. "He was devastated, Jewel. Hurt is a very tame word for what he went through. He loved Eric, considered him a son for two years. Can you imagine thinking a child is yours for that long? And then having him snatched away?"

She swallowed and lowered her gaze. "No, I can't imagine. It would devastate me too."

"Perhaps you can understand now that he's told you about them."

She looked up again, braving Chrysander's stare. "That's just it. I want your help."

Chrysander's brows came together in confusion. "My help? With what?"

"Finding Eric."

"No. Absolutely not. I won't allow Piers to go through that all over again."

Jewel put her hand over Chrysander's when he turned to go back inside.

"Please. Hear me out. Part of the problem was that Piers never got to say good-bye. He never got any closure. His wound is still raw and bleeding. He's still grieving for that two-year-old he lost. His only memory of Eric is of the day she left with him, how Eric screamed and cried for him. Maybe if he could see him now it would help to ease some of that pain. I can only imagine that he's wondered over the years if Eric is happy, if he's well, if he's needed anything. If he saw that Eric wasn't hurting, maybe it would go a long way to healing the awful pain Piers feels."

"You would do this?" Chrysander asked. "You would willingly bring a child back into his life that he loved? Risk contact with a woman he once loved just to make him happy again?"

"Yes," she said huskily. "I would do anything to ease his hurt."

Chrysander studied her for a long moment. "You love my brother very much."

She closed her eyes and turned away. "Yes," she whispered. "I do."

"All right, Jewel. I will help you."

She grabbed his hand. "Thank you."

"I just hope when this is all over that my brother is still speaking to me," he said wryly.

She shook her head vigorously. "I'll tell him you had nothing to do with it. I'll take sole responsibility."

"My brother is a lucky man, I think."

"I just hope he thinks so," she said wistfully.

"Give him time. I have no doubt he'll figure it out."

Chrysander leaned forward and kissed her forehead. "I'll do some digging and let you know what I come up with."

Bella slipped out through the glass doors. "I'm afraid

we've held him off for as long as possible. I hope you're done, because Theron and Piers are convinced we're plotting some evil."

Chrysander chuckled. "Bella, I have no doubt that where you're concerned, it's absolutely true. I haven't forgotten that you dragged my wife into a tattoo parlor not so many months ago."

Jewel burst out laughing. "A tattoo parlor? You have to tell me about this, Bella. Did Chrysander have a heart attack?"

"He might have bellowed a bit loudly just before he dragged us out," Bella said with an innocent grin.

Jewel wrapped an arm around Bella in a show of loyalty.

"Just what we needed around here. Another woman to cause trouble," Chrysander said with a mock groan.

The door opened, and this time Marley came out with Theron and Piers on her heels. Both men wore expressions of suspicion as they surveyed Chrysander laughing with Bella and Jewel.

"Whatever he's said, don't believe a word," Theron said as he dragged Bella back against his side.

"Why do I gain the impression that my family is plotting against me?" Piers murmured as he went to stand at Jewel's side.

She wrapped her arms around him, hugging him close. Then she leaned up to brush her lips across his jaw. "You're being paranoid. Chrysander was just divulging all your family secrets."

Both Theron and Piers donned expressions of horror. Chrysander held up his hands. "Don't worry. I've told them nothing you'll be sorry for later."

"You mean there is dirt they'd be sorry for?" Bella asked. "Do tell. Theron always acts as if I'm the trouble-maker in the family."

Jewel relaxed against Piers and enjoyed the laughing and teasing that went on between the others. She already liked Bella and Marley so much, and she was beginning to lose her uneasiness around Theron and Chrysander. To their credit, both men had seemingly accepted her presence in Piers's life.

Piers's hand went to her belly as it often did, rubbing lightly over the swell. She wasn't even sure he realized what he was doing, but it made her heart ache with love for him.

She was beginning to realize that for all his coldness and aloofness that he was a man of great passion. When he loved, he did so with everything he had. How fortunate both her and her child would be to have his love and devotion. She would never have to worry about being alone or of being accepted again.

"Are you ready for dinner, *yineka mou?*" he murmured close to her ear. "I have it on good authority that the chef has prepared all your favorites tonight."

"Hmmm, I think I could get used to being so spoiled," she said with a sigh.

"You're easily satisfied," he teased.

"I just want you," she said seriously.

Fire blazed in his eyes, and his grip tightened around her midsection.

"Don't tempt me so or I'll forget we have guests and take you upstairs to bed."

"And this would be bad why? Your brothers all have wives. Surely they'd understand."

He laughed and kissed her on the nose. "You're bad for my control, *yineka mou.* Come, let's go eat. I'll carry you up to bed later."

Seventeen

"Mrs. Anetakis, there is a call for you."

Jewel looked up to see the maid holding the cordless phone out to her. She took it and smiled her thanks at the younger woman. After she'd retreated, Jewel put the phone to her ear.

"Hello?"

"Jewel, this is Chrysander. I have some information for you about Eric. I'm glad you asked me to look into this. The news is not good."

Jewel frowned and got up from her seat at the breakfast table on the terrace. She ducked back inside so she could better hear over the distant roar of the ocean.

"What's wrong?"

"I found him. He's in foster care. He was made a ward of the state of Florida two years ago. He's been through six homes in that time."

"Oh no. No, no, no," she whispered. Her fingers curled tightly around the phone as she battled tears. This would destroy Piers.

"Jewel, are you all right?"

She swallowed the knot in her throat. Memories that she'd spent her life suppressing boiled to the surface.

"I'm okay," she said shakily. "Thank you for doing this, Chrysander. I'd appreciate it if you could e-mail me all the information you have. I want to thoroughly investigate this before I tell Piers."

"I understand. I'll send it over as soon as we get off the phone. And Jewel, if you need any further help from me, let me know."

"Thanks, Chrysander. How is Marley doing?"

Chrysander sighed. "It's been difficult for her. She's already ill with the pregnancy, and the stress of having to identify the kidnappers and give more statements is getting to her."

"I'm sorry," she offered softly. "Will you be much longer in New York? Will she have to remain there for the trial?"

"Not if I can help it," he said fiercely. "The District Attorney has offered a plea bargain. If they accept it, then they'll forego a trial, and Marley will be finished with this nightmare."

"Give her my love, please."

"I will. Let me know if there is anything else I can do."

"I will, Chrysander."

She hung up the phone and then went to find her laptop. A few minutes later, she received Chrysander's e-mail. She frowned as she read through the details. A few phone calls would have to be made, but she couldn't wait to tell Piers what she'd discovered. There was no need for

Eric to be in foster care when he had a family all too willing to take him in.

Piers sank into his chair behind his desk and looked ruefully at the piles of mail in front of him. Never before had he been so lax when it came to work matters. He had Jewel to thank for his inattention lately.

His e-mails were in the hundreds, his voice mail had reached capacity, and he hadn't opened mail in several days. His brothers would give him hell, but they'd also be happy to know that work wasn't his life any longer.

With a sigh, he powered up his computer so he could sift through the backlog of e-mails. Then he reached for his phone and turned on the speaker so he could weed through voice mails. Most were routine reports from various construction projects. A few minor emergencies from panicked hotel managers, and one offer to buy the new hotel in Rio de Janeiro. That one made him smile. There weren't many corporations that could afford one of the Anetakis's hotels. They spared no expense.

As soon as the voice mails were squared away, he dialed Chrysander's number. He wanted to check in on Marley and find out the results of their trip to New York to identify her kidnappers.

When he received no answer, he called Theron instead. They spent several minutes talking about business. Theron brought him up to speed on Chrysander and Marley and then conversation drifted back to business.

As he chatted, he idly sorted through the envelopes piled on his desk. When he got to one addressed to him from the laboratory that had performed the paternity test, he froze.

"I'll speak to you later, Theron. Give Bella my love."

He hung up and stared at the envelope in front of him. A smile eased his face as he fingered the seal. Here would be the proof of his paternity. In black and white, irrefutable proof that he was a father.

Last time it had gone the other way, and he'd lost everything that mattered most to him. This time…this time it would be perfect. He had a daughter on the way. His child.

Mine.

The surge of possessiveness that rocketed through his body took him by surprise.

He tossed the envelope aside. There was no need to open it. He knew what it would say. His trust in Jewel also surprised him, but he realized he did indeed have faith in her. He trusted her not to betray him.

After sorting through a few more envelopes he glanced back over at the letter. He should open it and revel in the feeling. Then he could go find Jewel and make mad, passionate love to her.

The idea made him tighten with need.

He felt like celebrating. Maybe he'd take Jewel on a trip to Paris. She loved to travel, and her doctor had pronounced her fully recovered from her surgery. To be on the safe side, he could schedule a check-up and a sonogram. Then they could take the private jet. They could make love in Paris and then maybe go on to Venice. Take the honeymoon they hadn't been able to take when they'd gotten married.

He picked up the envelope again, smiling as he turned it over. He only hesitated a moment before tearing it open and unfolding the letter within.

He scanned the contents, the perfunctory remarks thanking him for his business, and finally he got to the bottom where the results were posted.

And he froze.

He read it again, sure that he'd missed something. But no, there it was in black and white.

He wasn't the father.

Icy rage flooded his veins, burning, billowing until he thought he would explode. Again. It had happened again, only this time it was different. So very different.

What had she hoped to accomplish? Would she, like Joanna, wait for him to form an attachment to the child before leaving? Use the child as a bargaining tool?

Was Kirk the father or was he yet another man she dangled from her fingertips like a windup toy?

Older and wiser? He wanted to puke at his stupidity. In his arrogance, he'd imagined that he'd never be deceived as he'd been in the past, but what had he done to prevent it?

He looked down at the offending document again. His hands were shaking too much to keep it still. Damn her. Damn her to hell.

She'd wormed her way into his life, into his family's lives. His sisters-in-law loved her, and his brothers had accepted her. Because of him. Because he'd brought her into their unsuspecting midst.

Never had he felt so sick. He wished he'd never opened the damn thing.

What a fool he'd been. What a fool he'd always be. All this time wasted on building a relationship that was based on lies and treachery. He'd bought the house of her dreams, done everything in his power to make her happy.

And worse, he'd bought into the fantasy as well. He'd begun to believe that they could be a family. That he'd been gifted another chance at a wife and child. That he'd finally been given hope.

He stared bleakly at the paper in his hand. The worst part was he had to have played right into her hands by offering her a settlement regardless of her child's paternity. She won either way. And him? He'd lost everything.

Jewel clutched the printouts to her chest and hurried to Piers's office. She knew it would hurt him to find out Eric's fate and that Joanna had abandoned him two years ago, but the most important thing was getting Eric out of his current situation.

Nausea rose in her throat at the thought of the young boy in so many foster homes. Had he harbored the same hopes she had when she was a little girl, only to be disappointed over and over?

She didn't knock but burst through the door, breathless from her pace. She stopped abruptly when she saw Piers sitting at his desk, a document crumpled in his hand, his expression so horrible that she nearly forgot why she'd come.

"Piers?"

He turned his cold gaze to her, and she shivered as a chill washed up her spine.

She took a step forward. "Is everything all right?"

He rose slowly with calculated precision. "Tell me, Jewel. How did you think you would get away with it? Or did you just want to prolong the truth until you had me completely wrapped around your finger?"

Her heart sank. How had he found out about Eric? Why was he so angry?

"I was on my way to tell you now. I thought you'd want to know."

He laughed but the sound was anything but joyous. It skittered abrasively over her skin, and she shrank away from his obvious anger. Rage. That was the word for it. He vibrated with it.

"Oh yes, Jewel. I wanted to know. Preferably when this whole charade began. Did you enjoy hearing me spill my guts about Joanna and the deception she perpetrated? Did it give you satisfaction to know that yours was even more sound?"

She shook her head in confusion. What was he talking about?

"I don't understand. Why are you so angry? And at me? I didn't do this, Piers."

He gaped incredulously at her. "You didn't lie to me? You didn't try to foist another man's child off on me? You amaze me, Jewel. How you manage to sound the victim. The only victim here is me and the poor child you're pregnant with."

Hurt crashed over her, making her fold inward in a familiar defense mechanism she'd perfected over the years.

"You hate me," she whispered.

"Are you suggesting that I could love someone like you?" he sneered.

He thrust the paper forward. "Here is the truth, Jewel. The truth you never saw fit to give me. The truth I deserved."

She took the paper with a shaking hand, tears obscuring her vision. It took her three times to make sense of the words and when she realized what it said, she went surprisingly numb.

"This is wrong," she said in a low voice.

Piers snorted. "You'd still keep up the pretense? It's over, Jewel. These tests don't lie. It states with absolute certainty that there is no chance I could be the father of your child."

She stared up at him, tears trickling down her cheeks. He was cold. So cold. Hard. And unforgiving.

"You've waited for me to fall," she choked out. "You've been waiting for this since the day I called you. It's the only outcome that was acceptable to you. You weren't going to be satisfied until you proved I was no better than Joanna."

"You have quite a flair for dramatics."

She scrubbed angrily at her tears, furious that she'd allowed him to make her cry. "The results are wrong, Piers. This is your child. *She* is your child."

Something flickered in his eyes at her vehemence, but then he blinked, and it was gone, replaced with ice.

There would be no convincing him. He'd already tried and convicted her. She had some pride. She wouldn't beg. She wouldn't humiliate herself. She'd never allow him to know how shattered she was by his rejection. Or how much she loved him.

She lifted her chin and forced herself to stare evenly at him, steeling herself until she could no longer feel the shards of pain that pelted her.

"Someday you'll regret this," she said quietly. "One day you'll wake up and realize that you threw away something precious. I hope, for your sake, you don't take too long and that one day you can find the happiness you're so determined to deny yourself and others around you."

She turned stiffly, her heart breaking under the weight of her pain. She gripped the papers she'd intended to show Piers and held them close to her chest as she walked away. He made no effort to stop her, and she knew he wouldn't. He'd stay here, holed up in his refuge until she'd gone.

Methodically she took the stairs to the master bedroom. She got out a suitcase and began putting her clothing inside.

"Mrs. Anetakis, is there something you need?"

Jewel turned to see the maid standing in the doorway wearing a perplexed look.

"Could you arrange for a car to take me into town?" Jewel asked. "I'll be ready in fifteen minutes."

"Of course."

Jewel turned back to her packing, willing herself not to break down into more tears. She would survive this. She had survived worse.

When she had packed everything she thought she'd need, she smoothed out the papers that had all the information about Eric. No matter that she and Piers were no longer together, she couldn't allow that child to remain in the system, unwanted and tossed from family to family.

She closed her eyes and sighed. This would be so much easier with the money and power of the Anetakis name. Slowly she opened her eyes again and frowned. She may not have the money but she did have the name. Yes, Piers had provided a settlement for her in the case of a divorce, but who knows how long it would take to lay hands on it. She needed money now. Eric couldn't wait.

She went to her dresser and pulled out the diamond necklace and earrings Piers had given her on her wedding day. With one fingertip, she stroked the brilliant stones, remembering the way he'd fastened the necklace at her nape.

Between her engagement ring and the necklace and earrings, she should be able to raise enough cash to rent a place in Miami. But she'd need enough money to remain solvent until she would collect her settlement from Piers.

"Mrs. Anetakis, the car is ready for you."

Jewel closed her suitcase and smiled her thanks. She looked one more time around the room she'd shared with Piers and then walked down the stairs behind the maid.

When she was settled into the car, she directed the

driver to take her to the airstrip. She didn't have time to call for Piers's jet, though she didn't have any qualms about using it. She had no desire to be stuck here in this place for any longer than necessary. She'd take the first flight off the island, and go to New York to see Bella and Marley and pray that they'd help her save Eric.

Eighteen

"Jewel, what on earth are you doing here?" Bella asked as she all but dragged Jewel inside the doorway. "Does Piers know you're here? Did he come with you?"

Jewel swallowed the knot in her throat. Damn if she was going to get all weepy again.

Marley appeared behind Bella, her face soft with sympathy.

"What happened?" Marley asked.

Despite her resolve, Jewel burst into tears. Bella and Marley flanked her, each wrapping an arm around her as they guided her into Bella's living room.

"Are Chrysander and Theron here?" she managed to ask around her sobs.

"No, and they won't be back for a while," Bella said soothingly. "Now sit down before you fall over. You look dead on your feet."

Jewel perched on the edge of the couch while the other women took a seat on either side of her.

"What has that idiot brother-in-law of mine done?" Marley asked grimly.

Jewel tried to smile through her tears at Marley's show of loyalty. "I'm afraid he'd say it was what I'd done to him."

Bella snorted. "With that man, I'd hardly believe that. Besides, it's easy to see that you're crazy in love with him."

Jewel buried her face in her hands. "That's just it. He believes the absolute worst of me."

Marley put a hand on her shoulder and squeezed. "Tell us what happened."

With little reluctance, Jewel spilled the entire sorry tale from start to finish, including the part about Joanna and Eric and the paternity results.

"What an idiot," Bella said scornfully. "Did he even call the laboratory to double-check the results? Did he question them at all? Clearly there was some mix-up at the lab."

Jewel gave her a watery smile. "Thank you for believing in me. But the thing is, he got what he was waiting for. He's been waiting since the start for me to fall off the pedestal, so to speak. He hasn't been able to believe in a woman since Joanna."

"So what are you going to do?" Marley asked. "You're in love with him."

"But he doesn't love me. Moreover, he doesn't want to love me. I can't live with someone who distrusts me as much as he distrusts me."

"What about Eric?" Bella questioned. "Surely you won't leave him in his current situation."

"No," Jewel said fiercely. "And that's why I've come. I need your help."

Marley put her hand on Jewel's. "Anything."

"I pawned the jewelry that Piers gave me. It's enough to rent a small place in Miami so I can set up a permanent residence. But I'll need enough money socked away that the state will see me as a stable, financially able parent for Eric. I won't get a settlement from Piers until the divorce, and I have no idea how long that will take."

Bella grinned. "The lovely thing about having my own money, is that I don't need to rely on the Anetakis billions. No offense, Marley."

"None taken," Marley said dryly.

"I have some cash on hand that I can give you, and I'll wire you more funds so that you can rent something a little better than a 'small place' in Miami. If small is good, then bigger is better, right?"

Jewel squeezed both women's hands. "Thank you so much. I was so worried that you'd hate me, that you'd believe that I'd deceived Piers."

Marley sighed. "I have a feeling that Piers is going to wake up one day and realize he's made the worst mistake of his life. I almost wish I was there to see it."

"Don't feel so bad, Jewel," Bella said soothingly. "I'm afraid all of the Anetakis men are rather dense when it comes to love."

"So true," Marley agreed.

"You'll keep us posted on how things go with Eric? I'd love to meet him," Bella said.

"Of course I will."

"Do you have travel arrangements for your trip to Miami?" Marley asked.

Jewel shook her head. "Not yet. I've barely had time to breathe. I came straight here from the island."

Bella stood, her expression one of take charge. "First things first. We're going to go have a nice girly lunch followed by an afternoon of complete pampering at the spa. God knows you pregnant women need it. Then we're going to arrange for a private jet to fly Jewel to Miami, and I'll have a driver waiting there to pick her up and take her wherever she needs to go. Piers may be a dumb ass, but you're still family."

Jewel burst into tears again, and Bella groaned.

"Is it any wonder I have no desire to procreate? Pregnancy turns women into hormonal messes."

Marley dabbed quickly at her eyes, and Jewel burst out laughing. Marley joined her, giggling through her tears and finally Bella joined them as well.

"Okay, enough sniffling. Let's get out of here before the men return. I'll leave them a note telling them I've taken Marley off for an afternoon of debauchery. They won't be the least bit surprised," Bella said with a grin.

"Promise me you'll both visit me in Miami," Jewel said fiercely. "I'll miss you both terribly. I've always wanted a family—sisters—and I couldn't ask for better sisters than you two."

"Oh, I'll visit," Marley promised. "I'll blame it all on Bella. It's my standard excuse and keeps me out of trouble with Chrysander. Theron loves her so much that he's frighteningly indulgent with her."

"You're both very lucky," Jewel said wistfully.

Marley gave her a stricken look. "I'm so sorry, Jewel. That was incredibly thoughtless of me."

"Blame it on the pregnancy," Bella said. "Surely having a parasite inside you sucking all your brain cells has to negatively impact you sooner or later."

Marley and Jewel both cracked up.

"You're so delightfully irreverent," Jewel teased. "It's no wonder Theron loves you so."

"Come on, let's go, let's go. My man radar tells me the menfolk will be home soon. The more distance we put between here and where we're going, the less likely they'll be able to track us down."

They linked arms and headed out the door only to be stopped by Reynolds, Theron's head of security.

Bella sighed and cast a baleful look in the man's direction. "Can we count on you for a little discretion or will you break your neck reporting to Theron?"

Reynolds cleared his throat. "That will depend on where you think you're going."

Marley pressed forward. "What we have here, sir, is a damsel in distress. A very pregnant damsel in distress. She is in sore need of a day at the spa. You know, where we do all those frightening girly things that scare the devil out of men."

Reynolds swallowed and paled slightly. "Well as long as it's that and not a more inappropriate place."

Bella glared at him as she walked by him to the car. "You're never going to let me live down that strip club are you?"

"Strip club?" Jewel asked. "This I've got to hear."

"And I'll tell you all about it once we're wrapped in mud from head to toe," Bella said as they got into the car.

Bella leaned forward as Reynolds got into the front seat. "There's one more thing, Reynolds. This is top secret stuff. You didn't see Jewel, don't know who she is, never saw her in your life, *capiche?*"

Reynolds nodded solemnly. "Who?"

Bella smiled in satisfaction and leaned back in the seat once more.

"He's really an okay guy when he doesn't have a corncob wedged up his arse."

"I heard that," Reynolds commented.

Bella grinned and winked at the other two women.

"Okay girls, a day at the spa it is. Then we'll get Jewel to the airport and on her way to Miami."

Piers stared broodingly into the surf, hands shoved into the pockets of his trousers—pants that he hadn't changed out of in three days. He looked and felt like he'd been on a monthlong bender. He hadn't showered or shaved. The staff avoided him like the plague, and when he did come into contact with them, they all glared at him with disapproving eyes. As if he'd been the one to drive her away.

And he had, in a way. He hadn't made it easy for her to stay. No, he hadn't asked her to leave in so many words, but what woman would stay with a man who'd been so cruel, so derisive?

He closed his eyes and inhaled the sea air that Jewel so loved. She loved the ocean like he loved her. Passionately.

Love was supposed to be without barriers or conditions. He'd never offered that to Jewel. He hadn't even offered his unconditional support. No, he'd demanded and she'd given. He'd taken and she'd offered.

What a bastard he was.

How was she supposed to have ever been able to tell him the truth when he made it impossible for her to do so? He'd all but told her that he'd toss her out without thought if he found out she'd lied.

And the truth was he didn't care.

He'd realized it the moment he'd found her gone. He didn't care if the baby was his biological child or not. Jewel was married to him, which meant both belonged to him. He would be the baby's father because it was what Jewel wanted. It was what *he* wanted.

He hadn't loved Eric any less even knowing that he wasn't his biological child. He already loved his daughter, and nothing would change that. He'd ruined his chance at having a family. A wife and a daughter. All because he'd been so sure Jewel was another Joanna.

Jewel was right. He'd been waiting for her to fail, for her to give him the ammunition he needed to destroy her because it beat him being destroyed a second time. She was right about another thing, and it hadn't taken him long to realize it. He'd destroyed something very precious.

"I love you, *yineka mou,*" he whispered. "I don't deserve your love, but I can give you mine. I can try to make up for the many wrongs I have done to you. Please forgive me."

Just saying the words he'd vowed never to give another woman freed something buried deep in his soul. He breathed deeply, as past hurts fell away, carried on the wind further out to sea. He'd allowed himself to be ruled by bitterness and anger for too long. It was time to let go and embrace his future with Jewel.

He turned and strode back to the stone steps leading up to the house. He began barking orders as soon as he stepped inside. At first he was met by cold resistance, until the staff figured out what it was he was doing. Then there was a flurry of activity as everyone stumbled over themselves to provide him what information they could.

"I called a car for her to drive her into town," one of the maids offered.

When the driver was summoned, he said he'd driven her to the small airport and carried her single bag inside.

Frustrated, Piers took the car to the airport to question the ticket agent, but not even the Anetakis name was able to yield him any results. No one would tell him what if any flight Jewel took—or to where.

Kirk.

The name shot back through his memory. Of course. She had often gone back to Kirk's apartment when she needed a place to stay. Surely that's where she would go. She seemed to trust this fellow, and there was genuine affection and concern between them.

He looked down in disgust. He couldn't go anywhere looking as he did right now. He'd likely be arrested for vagrancy.

On his way back to the house, he phoned his pilot and instructed him to be fueled and ready to depart within the hour.

He was going to find Jewel and bring her and their child back where they belonged. Home.

Nineteen

Piers stood outside the San Francisco apartment and knocked. A few moments later, the door opened, but it wasn't Jewel who stared back at him. It was Kirk.

"Is Jewel here?" Piers asked stiffly.

Kirk's eyes narrowed. "Why would she be here? Why isn't she with you?"

Piers closed his eyes. "I had hoped she'd come here. Do you have any idea where else she might go?" It galled him to ask for this man's help, but to find Jewel, he'd do anything.

"You better come in and tell me what the hell is going on," Kirk said.

Piers followed him inside and the two sat down in the living room.

"Spill it," Kirk said.

"I said some terrible things to her," Piers admitted. "I wasn't thinking straight. I was angry and I lashed out."

"About?"

Knowing he needed this man's help, Piers poured out the entire story from start to finish. Maybe if he seemed remorseful enough, Kirk wouldn't think he was a total bastard and give him any information he had on Jewel.

"You are a first-class jerk, aren't you? Jewel wouldn't lie about something like that. Did she ever tell you about her childhood? I'm guessing not or you wouldn't have shoveled that horse manure at her."

"What are you talking about?"

Kirk made a sound of disgust. "From the time her parents died when she was barely older than a toddler, she was shuttled from one foster family to another. The first few were merely temporaries as the state tried to place her in a more permanent environment. The first was a real gem of a family. The oldest son tried to abuse her. She told her case-worker, who thankfully believed her. So she was placed in another home, this time with another foster child, a girl about her age. What Jewel didn't know was that the family never had any intention of taking both girls. They took two so they could choose. And it wasn't Jewel they chose. So she lost a family she'd grown to trust and a sister she loved."

"*Theos*," Piers said through tight lips.

"Things started looking up when a couple who couldn't have children decided they wanted to adopt Jewel. She went to live with them. The adoption was nearly final when the mother discovered she was pregnant. After years of infertility, she'd stopped trying and now she was suddenly pregnant. They couldn't afford more than one child, and you can imagine which one they chose. Once again, Jewel was rejected."

Piers closed his eyes. Just as he'd rejected her and her baby.

"After that, she didn't believe in happy endings any longer. You might say she grew up fast. She went through the motions of the system until she was old enough to be out on her own. Since then she's moved around constantly, never settling in one place, never forging ties with people. Never having a home. She simply doesn't believe she deserves one."

Kirk stared hard at Piers. "You've taken the one thing from her guaranteed to hurt her the most. *If* you find her, don't expect her to welcome you back with open arms."

Piers stared back at the other man, his stomach churning. "If she contacts you will you let me know immediately? She's pregnant and alone. I need to find her so I can make this right."

Kirk studied him for a long moment before finally nodding. Piers handed him his card.

"Call me day or night. It doesn't matter."

Kirk nodded and Piers rose to leave.

"Where will you go now?" Kirk asked when he saw Piers to the door.

"To New York to see my brothers. Something I should have done already," Piers said grimly.

Piers knocked on his brother's door and waited with dread for it to open. He didn't like facing his brothers with his mistakes, and he liked asking for their help even less, but if it would get Jewel back, he'd do anything.

"Piers? What the devil are you doing here? Why didn't you call to let us know you were coming? And where's Jewel?"

Piers looked up, wincing at the barrage of questions coming from Theron.

"Can I come in?"

Theron stepped to the side. "Of course. We were just about to sit down for dinner. I have to say, you look awful."

"Thanks," Piers said dryly.

They walked into the formal dining room, and Chrysander, Marley and Bella all looked up. Only Chrysander seemed surprised. The two women were more subdued.

Chrysander's sharp gaze found him. "What's happened?" he asked bluntly.

"Jewel left me," he said bleakly.

Theron and Chrysander both began talking at once while the women merely exchanged glances and remained silent.

"That doesn't make sense," Chrysander said. "Not after she spent all that time—"

Marley cut him off with a sharp elbow to his gut. Then she frowned at him and shook her head. Chrysander gave her a curious look but remained silent.

Bella stood, her hands on her hips. "Why did she leave you, Piers?"

Her voice was deceptively soft. It reminded Piers of the reason men feared women so much to begin with.

"Bella, perhaps Piers would prefer not to tell us such private things," Theron suggested.

Marley raised an eyebrow. "He's here isn't he? He obviously wants our help. We deserve to know if he deserves it or not."

Piers winced. "If you want to know the truth, no, I don't deserve your help, but I'm asking for it anyway."

"Why?" Bella demanded.

Piers looked at both women. "Because I love her, and I made a terrible mistake."

"So you called the stupid lab and they figured out it was all a mistake then?" Marley said furiously.

Chrysander and Theron turned to Marley and Bella.

Marley flushed and cast an apologetic look at Bella, who merely shrugged.

"I haven't called the lab. I don't care about the bloody results. I love her and our child. I don't give a rat's ass who the biological father is. She's my daughter, and I don't plan to give her or Jewel up."

"Why do I get the impression that we're the only two without the faintest clue what the devil is going on?" Theron said to Chrysander.

"No, but I bet our lovely wives could fill us in," Chrysander said as he rounded on Bella and Marley.

Both women crossed their arms over their chests and pressed their lips together.

Frustration beat at Piers's temples. He walked past his brothers to stand in front of Marley and Bella.

"Please, if you know where she is, tell me. I have to make this right with her. I love her."

Marley sighed and glanced over at Bella.

"I might have helped her get a place in Miami," Bella hedged.

Chrysander's eyebrows went up. "But isn't that where…"

Marley shot him another furious glance.

"Where in Miami?" Piers said, ignoring the exchange between Marley and Chrysander.

"If you go down there and upset her again, I'll personally sic every member of Theron's security team on you," Bella threatened.

"Just tell me, Bella. Please. I need to see her again. I need to make sure she and the baby are all right."

"When I spoke to her yesterday, they were just fine," Marley said casually.

"It would appear that you and Bella have been very busy women," Chrysander said darkly.

Marley sniffed. "If things were left to you men, the world would be a disaster."

"I think we've been insulted," Theron said dryly.

Bella thrust the piece of paper she'd been writing on toward Piers. "Here's her address. She trusted me, Piers. Don't screw this up."

Piers hugged her quickly and kissed her on the cheek. "Thank you. I'll bring her back for a visit as soon as I can."

Jewel smoothed her hand over Eric's hair as he slept and smiled at how peaceful and innocent he looked. Tucking his blanket around him, she turned to tiptoe from his bedroom.

Once in the kitchen, she prepared a cup of decaf tea and sipped the soothing, warm brew.

Her arrival in Miami couldn't have come at a better time. Eric had been taken from his previous home and was awaiting placement along with several hundred other children. It had taken several days to complete the paperwork, have the home study and background checks, but Eric was finally hers.

At first he'd been silent and restrained. No doubt he thought his placement with her was as temporary as all his other ones. She didn't try to persuade him any differently. It would take time to win his trust.

The important thing was that he had a home now. Thanks to Bella's generosity, they both had a home.

After checking on Eric one last time, she went into the living room and settled into her favorite chair. Nights were difficult, when all was silent. She missed Piers and the easy companionship they'd developed.

She had nearly dozed off in her chair when the doorbell rang. She got up quickly so it wouldn't disturb Eric and went to look out the peephole. No one knew her here, and she was wary of anyone knocking on her door. Surely Social Services wouldn't pay a surprise visit at this time of night.

What she saw shocked her to the core.

Piers. Outside her door, looking worried and a little haggard.

With fumbling fingers, she unlocked the deadbolt and opened the door a crack.

"Jewel, thank God," he said. "Please, can I come in?"

Her grip tightened on the door as she stared through the crack. Anger, pain—so much pain—surged through her veins. What could he possibly have to say to her that hadn't already been said?

She steeled herself, opened the door just enough that she could see him and he could see her.

"I won't ask how you found me. It isn't important."

He started to interrupt, holding up one hand in a plea, but she shook her head.

"No, you've said enough. I let you say all those things, and I took it, but I don't have to now. This is my home. You have no rights here. I want you to leave."

Something that looked suspiciously like panic spasmed in his eyes.

"Jewel, I know I don't deserve even a moment of your time. I said and did unforgivable things. I wouldn't blame you if you never spoke to me again. But *please,* I'm begging you. Let me in. Let me explain. Let me make things right between us."

The sheer desperation in his voice unsettled her. She wavered on the brink of indecision, her anger warring with the desire to relent and let him through the door. He stared at her with tortured eyes and slowly, she stepped back and opened the door wider.

He was inside in an instant. He gathered her in his arms and buried his face in her hair.

"I'm sorry. I'm so sorry, *yineka mou.*"

He kissed her temple, then her cheek and then clumsily found her lips. He kissed her with such emotion that it staggered her.

"Please forgive me," he whispered. "I love you. I want you and our baby to come home."

She pulled away, holding onto his arms for support. "You believe she's yours?" She couldn't keep the bitterness or suspicion from her voice.

"I don't care who the biological father is. She's mine. Just as you are mine. We're a family. I'll be a good father, I swear it. I love her already, and I want us to be a family, Jewel. Please say you'll give me another chance. I'll never give you any reason to leave me again."

He gathered her hands in his, holding them so tightly that she was sure her fingers were bloodless.

"I love you, Jewel. I was wrong. So wrong. I don't deserve another chance, but I'm asking—no *begging*—for one because there's nothing I want more than for you and our daughter to come home."

She stood there, mouth wide open, trying to process everything he flung at her. He loved her. He still didn't think he was the father. He didn't *care* if he wasn't the father. He wanted her and the baby back.

Her throat swelled, and her nose stung as tears gathered in her eyes. How difficult must this have been for him, to come all this way, thinking that the baby wasn't his, but wanting them anyway, accepting them anyway.

She should be angry, but the results had confirmed his worst fears, and yet it didn't matter.

He'd humbled himself in front of her, made himself as

vulnerable as a man could make himself. She had only to look at the sincerity burning like twin flames in his eyes to know that he spoke the truth.

He loved her.

"You love me?"

She needed to hear it again. Wanted it so desperately.

"I love you so much, *yineka mou.*"

She shook her head. "What does that mean, anyway?"

"What does what mean?"

"Yineka mou."

He smiled. "It means my woman."

"But you called me that the first night we made love."

He nodded. "You were mine even then. I think I fell in love with you that very night."

Tears welled in her eyes, and she swallowed back the sob that clawed its way up her throat.

"Oh Piers. I love you so much."

She threw herself back into his arms, holding onto him as tightly as she could. He held her just as firmly, his hands stroking her hair. Then his palm slid down to cup her belly.

He trembled against her, his big body shaking with emotion. When he spoke, there was a betraying crack that told her how close he was to breaking.

"How is our child?"

She closed her eyes as tears slipped from the corners. Then she reached down to hold on to his wrist as she stepped away.

"She's yours, Piers. I swear it to you. I haven't slept with another man. Only you. Please tell me you believe me. I know what the tests said, but they were *wrong.*"

He stared back at her, hope lighting his eyes. He swallowed and then swallowed again. "I believe you, *yineka mou.*"

She closed her eyes and hugged him again, burying her face in his strong chest.

"I'm sorry for hurting you, Jewel. I won't do so again, you have my word."

"There is something I must tell you," she said quietly.

He stiffened against her and slowly drew away, his eyes flashing vulnerability.

"You should sit down."

"Just tell me. There is nothing we can't work out."

She smiled. "I hope you won't be angry at what I've done."

"We can fix it. Whatever it is. Together, *yineka mou.*"

She took his hands in hers as they sat on the couch. "I came to Miami to find Eric."

He went completely still. "Why?"

"I thought you needed closure. I thought if you could see him happy and well adjusted that you could carry that memory instead of the one where he screamed and cried as his mother took him away."

"And did you find him?"

There was anticipation in his voice that told her how eager he was to know of Eric's well-being.

"Yes, I found him," she said softly.

Her grip tightened around his hands.

"Joanna abandoned him two years ago."

"What?"

Anger exploded from him in a volatile wave. He bolted from the couch, his hands clenched into fists at his sides.

"Why didn't she bring him to me? She knew I loved him. She knew I'd take him in."

Jewel shook her head sadly. "I don't know, Piers. He was taken into foster care and has been there for the last two years."

"This must be rectified. I won't allow him to remain in foster care. Not like you were, *yineka mou*. I won't allow your pain to be his."

She stood beside him, touching his arm. "How did you know about me?"

Piers looked at her with such pain in his eyes. "Kirk told me when I went to San Francisco looking for you. *Theos*, Jewel. I am so shamed by the way I treated you."

"Piers, Eric is here," she said gently.

His mouth dropped open in shock. "Here?"

She nodded. "He's asleep in his bedroom. You see, I couldn't allow him to remain in foster care either. I knew how much he meant to you, and I know how painful my childhood was. I searched for Eric before we split up. It was why I came to your office that day. I was going to tell you that I'd found him and that he was in foster care. I thought we could both fly to Miami to get him."

He closed his eyes and let out a groan. "Instead, I drove you away, and you came here yourself to take care of him."

"He's here, and he very much needs a mother and a father."

"You would do this? You would take in a child that is not your own?" he asked.

"Isn't that what you plan to do? What you planned to do when you thought our daughter was not your own?"

He gathered her close in his arms, his body trembling against hers. "I love you, *yineka mou*. So much. Never leave me again. Not even if I deserve it."

She laughed lightly. "I won't. Next time, I'll stay and fight, which is what I should have done this time. You won't get rid of me so easily again."

"Good," he said gruffly. "Now let's go see our son."

Epilogue

"She's the most beautiful girl in the world," Piers said proudly as he held up six-week-old Mary Catherine for his brothers to admire.

"You can only say that because Marley is having another boy," Chrysander pointed out.

"Listen to them," Bella said in disgust. "Why is it that babies turn men's minds to mush?"

"I thought that was good sex," Marley said mischievously.

"Well, that too," Jewel said with a laugh.

Eric stood with the Anetakis men, looking absurdly proud of his little sister. Jewel's heart never failed to swell when she saw the love between father and son.

Eric's adoption had become final just two weeks before Mary Catherine had been born. A week later, Piers had received a frantic phone call from the laboratory that had performed the paternity test. They had, indeed, made a mistake and mixed up his results with someone else's. Piers had been horrified all over again over the fact that he'd blasted Jewel, but she reminded him that he'd taken her word on faith long before he knew the results were in fact in error. That was enough for her.

Bella had been quick to point out that all they'd needed to do was wait for Mary Catherine to be born because no one in their right mind would ever deny that she was an Anetakis through and through.

She was dark haired and dark eyed, and blessed with the olive complexion of her father. She was for all practical purposes a miniature Piers.

Jewel looked around at her family, all gathered at her home on the cliff overlooking the sea. There was so much happiness here. It was hard to believe at times that it was all hers. That she had a family. That she belonged. She and Piers had both been drifters for so long, but somehow they'd found their way to one another and had at long last found what mattered the most. A home.

"I'd like to propose a toast," Chrysander said as he raised his glass. "To the Anetakis wives. I've no doubt they'll keep us on our toes well into our old age, and I plan to enjoy every minute of it."

"Here, here," Theron said as he raised his own.

Piers turned to smile at Jewel, and she rose to stand by his side as they both looked down at the bundle in his arms. She put out her arm, and Eric snuggled against her side.

"I'd also like to propose a toast," Jewel said. "To Bella. May she give Theron a house full of girls all as beautiful and as sassy as she is."

"Bite your tongue," Bella said, but her eyes twinkled merrily.

Theron put his arm around his wife. "God help me if that is true. One Bella is all this world needs."

"I'd like to propose a toast to love and friendship," Marley said. She pulled Jewel and Bella away from their husbands and linked her arms around them both.

Jewel and Bella squeezed back.

"To love and friendship," they both echoed.

* * * * *

*Celebrate Harlequin's 60th anniversary
with Harlequin® Superromance®
and the DIAMOND LEGACY miniseries!*

*Follow the stories of four cousins as they come to terms
with the complications of love and what it means to be a
family. Discover with them the sixty-year-old secret that
rocks not one but two families in...
A DAUGHTER'S TRUST by Tara Taylor Quinn.*

*Available in September 2009 from
Harlequin® Superromance®*

RICK'S APPOINTMENT with his attorney early Wednesday morning went only moderately better than his meeting with social services the day before. The prognosis wasn't great—but at least his attorney was going to file a motion for DNA testing. Just so Rick could petition to see the child…his sister's baby. The sister he didn't know he had until it was too late.

The rest of what his attorney said had been downhill from there.

Cell phone in hand before he'd even reached his Nitro, Rick punched in the speed dial number he'd programmed the day before.

Maybe foster parent Sue Bookman hadn't received his message. Or had lost his number. Maybe she didn't want to talk to him. At this point he didn't much care what she wanted.

"Hello?" She answered before the first ring was complete. And sounded breathless.

Young and breathless.

"Ms. Bookman?"

"Yes. This is Rick Kraynick, right?"

"Yes, ma'am."

"I recognized your number on caller ID," she said, her voice uneven, as though she was still engaged in whatever physical activity had her so breathless to begin with. "I'm sorry I didn't get back to you. I've been a little…distracted."

The words came in more disjointed spurts. Was she jogging?

"No problem," he said, when, in fact, he'd spent the better part of the night before watching his phone. And fretting. "Did I get you at a bad time?"

"No worse than usual," she said, adding, "Better than some. So, how can I help?"

God, if only this could be so easy. He'd ask. She'd help. And life could go well. At least for one little person in his family.

It would be a first.

"Mr. Kraynick?"

"Yes. Sorry. I was…are you sure there isn't a better time to call?"

"I'm bouncing a baby, Mr. Kraynick. It's what I do."

"Is it Carrie?" he asked quickly, his pulse racing.

"How do you know Carrie?" She sounded defensive, which wouldn't do him any good.

"I'm her uncle," he explained, "her mother's— Christy's—older brother, and I know you have her."

"I can neither confirm nor deny your allegations, Mr. Kraynick. Please call social services." She rattled off the number.

"Wait!" he said, unable to hide his urgency. "Please," he said more calmly. "Just hear me out."

"How did you find me?"

"A friend of Christy's."

"I'm sorry I can't help you, Mr. Kraynick," she said softly. "This conversation is over."

"I grew up in foster care," he said, as though that gave him some special privilege. Some insider's edge.

"Then you know you shouldn't be calling me at all."

"Yes… But Carrie is my niece," he said. "I need to see her. To know that she's okay."

"You'll have to go through social services to arrange that."

"I'm sure you know it's not as easy as it sounds. I'm a single man with no real ties and I've no intention of petitioning for custody. They aren't real eager to give me the time of day. I never even knew Carrie's mother. For all intents and purposes, our mother didn't raise either one of us. All I have going for me is half a set of genes. My lawyer's on it, but it could be weeks—months—before this is sorted out. Carrie could be adopted by then. Which would be fine, great for her, but then I'd have lost my chance. I don't want to take her. I won't hurt her. I just have to see her."

"I'm sorry, Mr. Kraynick, but…"

* * * * *

Find out if Rick Kraynick will ever have
a chance to meet his niece.
Look for A DAUGHTER'S TRUST
by Tara Taylor Quinn,
available in September 2009.

We'll be spotlighting a different series
every month throughout 2009
to celebrate our 60th anniversary.

Look for Harlequin® Superromance®
in September!

*Celebrate with
The Diamond Legacy
miniseries!*

Follow the stories of four cousins as they come to terms
with the complications of love and what it means to
be a family. Discover with them the sixty-year-old secret
that rocks not one but two families.

A DAUGHTER'S TRUST by *Tara Taylor Quinn*
September

FOR THE LOVE OF FAMILY by *Kathleen O'Brien*
October

LIKE FATHER, LIKE SON by *Karina Bliss*
November

A MOTHER'S SECRET by *Janice Kay Johnson*
December

Available wherever books are sold.

www.eHarlequin.com

HSRBPA09

You're invited to join our Tell Harlequin Reader Panel!

By joining our new reader panel you will:

- Receive Harlequin® books—they are FREE and yours to keep with no obligation to purchase anything!
- Participate in fun online surveys
- Exchange opinions and ideas with women just like you
- Have a say in our new book ideas and help us publish the best in women's fiction

In addition, you will have a chance to win great prizes and receive special gifts!
See Web site for details. Some conditions apply.
Space is limited.

To join, visit us at
www.TellHarlequin.com.

Stay up-to-date on all your romance reading news!

The Harlequin Inside Romance newsletter is a **FREE** quarterly newsletter highlighting our upcoming series releases and promotions!

CELEBRATE 60 YEARS
OF PURE READING PLEASURE
WITH MORE EXCITING SERIES
SPOTLIGHTS, FEATURED
EVERY MONTH!

NEW YORK TIMES
BESTSELLING AUTHOR
DIANA PALMER
BRINGS YOU A
BRAND-NEW STORY!

CELEBRATE
MOTHER'S DAY
WITH HARLEQUIN®!

**Go to
eHarlequin.com/InsideRomance**
or e-mail us at
InsideRomance@Harlequin.com
to sign up to receive
your **FREE** newsletter today!

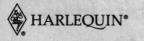

HARLEQUIN®

American ★ Romance®

The Ranger's Secret
REBECCA WINTERS

When Yosemite Park ranger Chase Jarvis rescues
an injured passenger from a downed helicopter,
he is stunned to discover it's the woman he
once loved. But Chase is no longer the man
Annie Bower knew. Will she forgive him for
the secret he's been keeping for ten long years?
And will he forgive Annie for her own secret—
the daughter Chase didn't know he had…?

*Available September
wherever books are sold.*

"LOVE, HOME & HAPPINESS"

www.eHarlequin.com

HAR75279

REQUEST YOUR FREE BOOKS!

2 FREE NOVELS PLUS 2 FREE GIFTS!

Silhouette®

Desire®

Passionate, Powerful, Provocative!

YES! Please send me 2 FREE Silhouette Desire® novels and my 2 FREE gifts (gifts are worth about $10). After receiving them, if I don't wish to receive any more books, I can return the shipping statement marked "cancel". If I don't cancel, I will receive 6 brand-new novels every month and be billed just $4.05 per book in the U.S. or $4.74 per book in Canada. That's a savings of almost 15% off the cover price! It's quite a bargain! Shipping and handling is just 50¢ per book.* I understand that accepting the 2 free books and gifts places me under no obligation to buy anything. I can always return a shipment and cancel at any time. Even if I never buy another book, the two free books and gifts are mine to keep forever.   225 SDN EYMS 326 SDN EYM4

Name	(PLEASE PRINT)	
Address		Apt. #
City	State/Prov.	Zip/Postal Code

Signature (if under 18, a parent or guardian must sign)

Mail to the Silhouette Reader Service:
IN U.S.A.: P.O. Box 1867, Buffalo, NY 14240-1867
IN CANADA: P.O. Box 609, Fort Erie, Ontario L2A 5X3

Not valid to current subscribers of Silhouette Desire books.

Want to try two free books from another line?
Call 1-800-873-8635 or visit www.morefreebooks.com.

* Terms and prices subject to change without notice. Prices do not include applicable taxes. Sales tax applicable in N.Y. Canadian residents will be charged applicable provincial taxes and GST. Offer not valid in Quebec. This offer is limited to one order per household. All orders subject to approval. Credit or debit balances in a customer's account(s) may be offset by any other outstanding balance owed by or to the customer. Please allow 4 to 6 weeks for delivery. Offer available while quantities last.

Your Privacy: Silhouette Books is committed to protecting your privacy. Our Privacy Policy is available online at www.eHarlequin.com or upon request from the Reader Service. From time to time we make our lists of customers available to reputable third parties who may have a product or service of interest to you. If you would prefer we not share your name and address, please check here. ☐

SDES09R

Silhouette DESIRE

COMING NEXT MONTH
Available September 8, 2009

#1963 MORE THAN A MILLIONAIRE—Emilie Rose
Man of the Month
The wrong woman is carrying his baby! A medical mix-up wreaks
havoc on his plans, and now he'll do anything to gain custody of
his heir—even if it means seducing the mother-to-be.

#1964 TEXAN'S WEDDING-NIGHT WAGER—
Charlene Sands
Texas Cattleman's Club: Maverick County Millionaires
This Texan won't sign the papers. Before he agrees to a divorce,
he wants revenge on his estranged wife. But his plan backfires
when she turns the tables on him....

#1965 CONQUERING KING'S HEART—Maureen Child
Kings of California
Passion reignites when long-ago lovers find themselves in each
other's arms—and at each other's throats. Don't miss this latest
irresistible King hero!

#1966 ONE NIGHT, TWO BABIES—Kathie DeNosky
The Illegitimate Heirs
A steamy one-week affair leaves this heiress alone and pregnant—
with twins! When the billionaire father returns,
will a marriage by contract be enough to claim his family?

#1967 IN THE TYCOON'S DEBT—Emily McKay
The once-scorned CEO will give his former bride what she
wants...as soon as she gives him the wedding night he's long been
denied.

#1968 THE BILLIONAIRE'S FAKE ENGAGEMENT—
Robyn Grady
When news breaks of an ex-lover carrying his child, this
billionaire proposes to his mysterious mistress to create a
distraction. Yet will he still want her to wear his ring when she
reveals the secrets of her past?

SDCNMBPA0809